Wrong
Victim
A NOVEL

TRINA ATOR ERNST

ISBN: 098864651X
ISBN-13: 978-0988646513 (A Zone Publishing)

DEDICATION

To all my friends and family.
You are the reason I am here...

CONTENTS

ACKNOWLEDGMENTS

Thanks for all your help. Iris O. You are a wonder.
Mark, thanks so much for your constant encouragement.

CHAPTER 1

Clunk! Janet listened to the box she had just mailed drop into the package drop-off slot at the post office. She stopped here a couple of times a week, a regular, and she was friendly with a lot of the staff. The people behind the desk were always very helpful with helping her find the cheapest way to send a package and, in Janet's mind, they got a bad rap for a few crazies and their supposed "going postal." Just to make sure that the package really went all the way through the box drop and into the room on the other side, Janet couldn't help herself and reopened the door to make sure the box wasn't stuck somewhere half way in the middle. "Stop that, Janet," she mentally chastised herself for checking and rechecking the drop box. OCD was somewhat of a problem for her, but really, she only had a slight problem with just a few things. Washing her hands maybe a little too often, checking and rechecking the stove to make sure she had turned it off after using it, and the iron… but it would be so easy to add a new obsession to the already bothersome collection she had. Janet really tried not to be so neurotic about whether she had done things or not. She really didn't need that extra craziness going on in her life now. Her family was already concerned that she was a bit too paranoid about everything.

A few months ago, Janet had been a real estate agent. Some of the other agents she met in the business were nice (they usually quit) but most of them would run you over in a heartbeat to get to a dollar bill on the sidewalk. She tried to avoid those people. But always, always they managed to stick their collective noses into her business, find out some tidbit of information about her, and then twist it around to make it sound like Janet was an idiot agent who had no idea what she was doing, or that she stole office supplies and handed them out on street corners for free, or whatever. Why they felt compelled to make up stories about her, Janet had no idea, but it had really started to bother her lately; and so finally, one day, out of the blue, it really got to be more than she could take. Janet had just had it. She packed up her things, jumped into her car, and never looked back.

Janet tended to think of that period in her life as the "dark times." I mean, she thought, what compelled her to stick around doing a job that paid crap money, where she had to drop whatever she was doing on any day of the week and drive around for something for someone that really could have been handled later. And to top that off, Janet had to associate daily with a couple of dislikable people.

Putting her gloves on as she walked out the glass doors of the post office, Janet thought to herself that fall was definitely here now in Delaware and the extra nip in the air was just enough that today she had finally dug out a pair of gloves. She was glad she had, because the heater in her car took forever to warm up. She was often at her destination just when her car had finally started to get warm. Janet clicked the unlock button on her key fob and her silver Hyundai beeped a little "hello" to her (or at least she imagined it was saying "hi.") It was just another tiny bit of happy to have a friendly sounding car.

Janet slid into the driver's seat and fastened her seatbelt. She had kind of left the house in a hurry today, barely glancing in the mirror before leaving, and it occurred to her that she might have raccoon eyes or lipstick teeth or something. She reached up, pulled down the visor, and gazed into the lighted vanity mirror. Not too bad, Janet thought to herself as she quickly wiped a little smudge of eyeliner from under her eye.

She had gotten into the habit of putting on makeup every day when she was a real estate agent. One day shortly after starting that, she realized that, hey, people treated you differently when you were nicely dressed, your hair was fixed into an actual style, your fingernails looked like pretty candy at the tips of your fingers, and you had always made certain that you had added just the right amount of matching accessories to your outfit. So, after quitting real estate, Janet tried to keep up most of the beauty things, but chose to forego the fake French tipped nails, as they were expensive and it hurt like hell to get them done. Besides, it was easier to do everyday things without them getting in the way.

Janet never really thought that she was good looking. She thought that maybe she *might* be a little bit better looking than average. At about 5' 3" and 115 pounds, she felt like she could stand to lose a few pounds. But all in all, she liked the way she looked. Janet was kind of proud of her long, dark shoulder-length hair, her brown eyes, and her darker skin tone. Coming from a small town in Montana, Janet had grown up around people whose ancestors had also homesteaded there. In her town, a large portion of the population had ancestors who were from Sweden, Norway, or Denmark. It seemed to Janet that every third person was tall and/or blonde. She always felt a little like the odd one out, with her Heinz 57 pedigree... some German, some Welsh, maybe French. She really didn't know which country or countries her ancestors had originated from. Janet guessed it just hadn't been that important to her family down through the years to keep up traditions. It was more important to work hard and become Americans. They were just small-town people who had small-town jobs and knew their neighbors well enough to just walk in the front (or back) door of someone's house and say "Hey, hello... it's Janet... anyone home?"

She missed the easy life of a small town for those little things mostly, but unfortunately, all the jobs were in the big cities; so she had eventually moved east, chasing a changing stream of jobs throughout her 42 years.

Janet fired up the Hyundai and quickly shut off the radio. She had been listening to it earlier, wanting to find out the weather for the day. Mostly, she enjoyed the quiet and the car ride and being alone with only her thoughts. It was good "me time," she thought, I'd better not waste it. After putting the car in gear and carefully backing out of her parking spot, Janet headed down Route 40 toward the bank. She had some checks she had to deposit and wanted to do it before the people who had sent the checks "accidentally" ran out of money. Janet felt like people who paid for purchases from her by check somehow always seemed to do that. Janet felt (stupidly she realized) that it only happened to her. She had always kind of felt as though she had a sign on her back that said "sucker," and that she always seemed to attract the flakey no-pay or slow-pay buyers on eBay or other auction sites. Even though that happened often enough, Janet sometimes still let people pay her by check. She hated to do it, but she always seemed to cave in and just let it happen. The trip to the bank was just one more errand to add to her list.

Janet pulled into the bank and found a spot a few rows from the front. She could have gotten a closer spot, but as she rarely exercised, any tiny bit more of walking would do her good. As she walked up to the entrance, Janet was pleased to see a man holding the door for her. He was not bad looking, Janet thought to herself, about her age, maybe a little younger, nice thick dark brown hair. She smiled and said a polite thank you, and he nodded his head and said, "My pleasure." It was always nice when someone took notice of you and stopped what they were doing to do a little kindness. She wished more people were like that.

Janet stopped in the entryway of the bank at the cash machine and the man who had held the door for her kept on going, into the bank and out of sight. Janet quickly put her ATM card into the machine and deposited the envelope with the checks into her checking account. She always filled out the deposit envelopes at home, preferring not to stand around a bank for any longer than she had to. Things happen.

After the ATM was done, it made a little ping sound and spit Janet's debit card back out of the slot. Janet fumbled with her bag a little, trying to put the deposit slip into it while at the same time trying to take out her keys. One thing at a time, Janet, she reminded herself. She was always trying to do too many things with one hand. Her other hand was always holding onto something that was next up after this task. It was an odd habit Janet was trying to break, because in reality, 99 percent of the time the next thing up was not something that really had to be done immediately afterwards. She always ended up dropping too much crap because of it.

Janet walked back to her car and hopped in, sighing in relief that she could now go home again. Sometimes, the world seemed just too big for her. Life and other people were too complicated, and she preferred to go out and about as little as possible more and more lately. At least this meant she spent less money on gas, which was not a bad thing. Janet put the car in gear and headed toward home.

Janet lived with her husband Eddie in a quiet suburban neighborhood, just far enough out that the traffic had thinned to just a few cars as she had finally reached the corner where she had to make a left onto the road toward her house. She and Eddie had bought the house from a builder, seriously enjoying the luxury of finally being able to pick and choose the features they wanted for their brand new home. That was several years ago, though, and their house was getting a little run down. Both she and Eddie were practical people and therefore reluctant to update their house with new things when the old things were perfectly fine and still worked. Meanwhile, her neighbors had poured lots of money into their homes, putting in new kitchens and redoing bathrooms, adding wood floors and stripping the "free with purchase" shrubs from their front lawns, replacing them with finely cut shrubs and white gravel in their garden beds. Her neighbors always seemed to make sure that their lawns always looked freshly cut. On top of that, their grass was always way too green! As Janet drove into her driveway, she looked at their lawn and thought to herself, yeah, it was green now. But that was just because the particular weed that had taken over most of the lawn seemed to grow and thrive in the recent dry conditions.

Janet grabbed her purse and headed into the house. It wasn't that Janet didn't want to have a neat and tidy house with all the newest stuff and new paint and appliances; it was just... can't someone else just do it for us? Janet just felt too busy with her art and her crafts and reading and trying to sell stuff online. Cleaning (which in Janet's mind was a never-ending gerbil wheel of doom) just never seemed like top priority in her daily life. That is, until someone thinks they will "drop on over" unannounced. Christ, if people saw how I really lived, Janet thought, they would probably think I was a brain case. Which, she guessed, she probably could be.

Janet opened the front door and walked into the entryway. It wasn't her dream home. There were things from the very start that she didn't like. However, at some point you have to compromise with the amount of money you have to spend, with what your spouse thinks, and what you really want, which never adds up to "all my dreams have finally come true." Janet truly believed that she was lucky with what she had. In some ways, her dreams had come true. She had a loving husband, two awesome kids, and a nice house in a nice neighborhood. All the same, she always felt like something was missing. Friends.

She just wasn't that good at keeping friendships very long. People, she had found out, were just like her. They only wanted to talk about themselves, do what they wanted to do, and only when they wanted to do it. It was just too much work to find and then to maintain new friendships. Janet was still good friends with the people she had grown up with. In fact, she was still closer to her old friends than she was with almost anyone she had met since living on the East Coast. There was something about shared lives growing up and a small community that cemented a bond of friendship that a newly minted one had a hard time doing. Oh well.

As Janet walked into the house and turned on the foyer light, nobody ran to the door to greet her. She hadn't really expected anyone to be waiting at the door. Her kids were now long past that age; that was just the way her life was now and that was okay with her. Anyway, even after a short time out in the world, Janet felt as if she needed to decompress a little bit after returning home before talking to anyone. Her family knew that and really tried to give her the space she needed.

Her son Robbie, who was twenty, pretty much kept to himself in his own room. While he was extremely smart, he was not yet up to the point in his life job-wise where he felt he should be. For now, he was happy still living at home until he could find and afford his own place. Janet was sure that would happen soon.

It was almost the same thing for Gabrielle, her daughter. Gabby had started out her young life calling everyone and anyone she met a friend, but now she really had only a few people that she called true friends. Her definition of people she thought of as friends had lately changed, and for the better. Now, Gabby seemed to finally recognize that the people who were her real friends were the ones who stuck by her during hard times—and that the majority of the people she knew were just friendly acquaintances. Still, even with occasional visits to local hangouts with her friends, Gabby did most of her daily communication with friends she had met online, people who had the same interests and passions that she did.

Eddie and Janet were sometimes concerned that Gabby wasn't getting out enough, but they were hoping that, like Robbie, she would soon find her place in the world. Luckily for them, Janet didn't feel like she was a Mrs. High Pressure Mom. She gave them the space they needed to grow, she loved them, and she even liked them and wanted to be around them (when they let her). Janet knew her almost perfect life would change some day, but until then she enjoyed it for now, immensely.

Eddie, what could she say about Eddie? He had always been a hard worker, with a great work ethic. Janet thought it was nice to have a husband who loves what he does and is happy in his job. Lately, however, the kind of research that Eddie so loved to do wasn't as popular as it had been, and of course, there had been layoffs. Unfortunately, Eddie had lost a job he loved in a round of layoffs, and afterwards there were some tough times for them. Eddie networked and quickly found another great job that sounded extremely interesting to him; it just didn't pay quite as well. Janet had tried to cut back as best she could when their economic situation had changed, but seriously... shopping is shopping. Even if your house is so full of stuff you couldn't possibly stuff another thing in to it, Janet had found that compulsive shopping for her, as for many people she knew, had become her preferred form of therapy.

Janet went into the living room and threw her purse down on the couch. Her cat, CooCoo, quickly came up and rubbed her head along the sides of Janet's legs. Cats were great; they always seemed to know when you most needed love. Janet had always had cats growing up, but CooCoo was special. She was just simply a sweet loving cat. Who couldn't love that?

Janet had a few moments alone, relaxing on the couch and petting CooCoo, before Robbie and Gabrielle showed up, looking to see if Mom had gotten them anything while she was out and then to ask her about what was for dinner. Why are they asking me? Janet thought to herself. They can microwave a box from the freezer just as easy as I can. But Janet figured that, just like she did, they thought food tasted better when someone else had made it.

The rest of the evening and the night would be filled with the normal stuff: feed the cat, and then feed herself and the kids whatever sounded good to them at the time. Eddie would come home a while later and make himself whatever he wanted to eat. There would be a brief discussion about what each of their days had been like, and after that, everyone would all wander off into their own little corners of the house and continue with what they had been doing earlier. Since the kids had gotten older, Janet thought they were almost like a bunch of related roommates. That was all the kids really seemed to want now; but Janet knew things would change—they always did.

Catching up on the news on the computer that evening, Janet saw that there had been a bank robbery nearby today—at the same freaking bank she had gone to! It must have happened right after she left. Oh my god, see! I knew something like this would happen, Janet thought to herself. No one was hurt, but the bank robbers—there were two of them—had carried guns. Or at least a gun. The article wasn't clear. But they did get away with some money, around about $6000, the article said. Jeez, Janet thought. I'm glad I left when I did. That could have been me lying on the floor with my hands over my head. I would have peed my pants, no doubt about it.

CHAPTER 2

The next couple of weeks were hectic ones for Janet. She had recently decided to sell a bunch of her many "collections" of things, various assortments of odd stuff that continued to grow as she kept adding to the hoard, because hey, that was what collectors did. The "collections" were already overrunning every extra inch of room in the non-living areas and were now verging on taking over all of the rest of the room in the house. She was constantly taking pictures, writing descriptions, and listing her stuff for sale on different places on the Internet. It was hard for her to sell some things, because they just never seemed to sell for as much as she had originally paid for them. Janet rationalized that her enjoyment of the item while she owned it was worth the difference. Still, it was hard parting with stuff she had once "just had to have."

Janet was in the middle of a giant ball of tape, trying to salvage some of it that she had clumsily taped to itself while trying to seal a package when her cell phone rang. Trying and then failing to un-stick the mass of tape from her hands before reaching for the phone, she finally gave up and picked up the cell phone, her hands still covered with the tape.

"Hello," Janet said, without even checking the screen to see who was calling, because she was still struggling to get the tape to go where it was supposed to go on the package.

The voice on the other end of the phone paused for a second before speaking.

"Hi, I hope you don't think this is weird, but, do you remember that bank robbery a couple weeks ago at the RCM Bank? It happened sometime in the middle of the business day when the bank was open. Well, I'm the guy who held the door open for you at the entrance. You stayed at the cash machine and I went into the bank and then it got robbed?"

Janet put down the package she was working on and replied cautiously to the voice on the phone.

"Um, so you're the guy who held the door open for me, right before the bank was robbed? Um, how did you get my number? And for that matter, my name?"

The voice on the other end responded with a nice-sounding laugh.

"Before you say anything else, I want to explain. I have been thinking of you... this is so not coming out right... not in some weird sicko way or anything, but since that day—that day that will be forever etched in my brain—thinking I knew you from somewhere. Then I finally remembered where I had seen your face before. You sell real estate. For a while I've been seeing your picture in the paper and on signs around town."

"Oh," Janet sat back feeling like she could relax a bit. She had gotten several of these calls since quitting real estate—apparently, she had moved on in the world, but the world of the Internet hadn't. She still saw her name pop up on Zillow and other home search sites as a person to contact about area homes for sale. "Well, I hope you aren't calling about real estate, are you?" Janet said as she shifted the phone from one ear to the other. "'Cuz I quit doing that a while ago. But I could recommend someone for you if you like."

"Oh, I hadn't realized. I'm sorry for bothering you then. See, I am thinking about selling my house fairly soon and moving to a smaller place in a new area… and so I was looking on Zillow for a real estate agent and saw your picture and your name, and then I realized why you had looked so familiar. You do know that your name is still on that site?"

Janet climbed up off the floor, her favorite place to do any sort of wrapping or art or anything and sat down in a nearby chair.

"Oh, yes… Zillow. Do you have any idea how hard it is to get your name out of the real estate system? I think it must be like the mob, you know, 'once you get in, you never get out.' Janet laughed, just a tad sarcastically, because she really wished she could wipe that strange part of her life out of her mind forever.

The voice on the other end chuckled a little along with her. Then, there was an awkward pause for a moment before Janet realized that she finally remembered seeing the guy before.

"Oh my god, so were you in the bank when the bank robbery happened?" Janet heard a brief sigh from the man on the other end of the phone.

"Yes, unfortunately."

"Oh my god! You must have been scared to death. I would have been. Are you okay now?" Janet shifted her phone again and sat forward a little bit so her cell phone reception was better.

"Well, now I'm okay. But at the time, um... I have to admit I was a little scared. Having men waving guns around like they were just Fourth of July sparklers and then being forced to lay on the floor with my hands on my head... not my idea of a lot of fun."

Janet smiled to herself. She liked his sense of humor. Her favorite type of person was one who could find the humor in the worst sort of situation. Sometimes that was the only way a person could preserve their sanity.

"Well, I'm glad you're okay. That was just too weird. See, that is why I hate banks. Oh, and the fact that they overcharge for everything." As she paused to take a breath, Janet thought she heard a small snort from the other end of the phone. "So, would you like me to recommend a real estate agent for you? I have a few that I know who are awesome and honest and fun to work with."

The voice on the other end paused for a second. "Well, I'm kind of sorry, or maybe glad for you, that you aren't in the house business anymore. You are kind of funny and you sound like a nice person. You seem just like the kind of person I would want to have selling my house. But then again, maybe it is a good thing that you aren't in real estate anymore. With the market today the way it is, it's a crapshoot. I have no idea what to do... sell, move out and rent, stay put, should I do some updates? It would be nice to be able to talk to someone knowledgeable about the subject, and also someone who isn't trying to "sell me on" something at the same time would be great." The voice on the other end continued, a little hesitantly.

"This might be too much to ask, and don't be afraid to say no, but... maybe you would like to meet me for coffee at the Starbucks on Route 40 and we can talk, and you can advise me informally about what I should do about my house. In return, I could tell you all the gory details about the bank robbery, if you're interested. I would buy the coffee… and I might even spring for a muffin or something."

Janet paused. Seriously, she was a little taken aback by the guy's request. What if this person were some kind of nut who was going to chop her up into pieces and dump her in the ocean? She didn't even know his name. And Eddie… Eddie would think she was crazy for doing this. Eddie also was kind of a jealous person and he really didn't like to see Janet talking to other men, even if it was only part of her doing business. In the past, it had really made it hard for her to do her job. She was glad that now she was out of the real estate game, the stress level in the house had gone down considerably. Still, Janet thought… it would be nice to feel free to talk to anyone, male or female. Sometimes she felt so lonely. But she really didn't want to make Eddie unhappy.

After a few seconds of thought, and before she actually knew what she was saying and/or that she even was going to say it, she blurted out, "Well, I don't even know your name! How do I know you won't make me swim with the fishes? You could be a crazy for all I know."

"David," said the voice on the other line, laughing. "My name is David Farmer. And no, I'm not a farmer. Or a crazy person. I work in the IT business, you know, geeky computer stuff. You can check me out online if you want. I'm clean. I really have nothing to hide… except for maybe my abysmal housecleaning skills. That, no one needs to know about."

Janet laughed. Ah, a kindred spirit, one who was also a messy housekeeper. "Well, David, if that *is* really your name, I suppose I could meet you for a free coffee. And really, Starbucks seems harmless enough. Even though I'm glad to be out of the real estate business, I do still enjoy some parts of the real estate job. And, truth be told, I really want to hear about that bank robbery. That still really freaks me out, even though I had already left the bank went it happened. Too close."

"Cool!" David said on the other end. "Any time this week would be great. How about Wednesday at 11 a.m.?"

Janet searched her brain to remember if she had anything going on that day. Yeah right, as if she were having tea with the Queen or something. She never did anything, actually; in fact, she rarely left the house lately except to run errands.

"This Wednesday at 11 a.m. at the Starbucks on 40? That sounds okay with me. I have cleared my schedule just for you," she laughed hysterically. He must think she was mad. "I really have no life, so any time or day would be great for me."

"Okay, well, I will see you then. I think I will be still able to recognize you, unless you've grown an arm out of your forehead or something. If you forgot what I look like, just look for a man with brown hair, wearing a light blue jacket, and drinking a giant coffee while staring out into space."

Janet smiled. "I think I remember what you look like. If not, I will just walk up to anybody and everybody and ask them, "Are you David?" I don't mind looking stupid. It's my gift."

"You say the funniest things," David said on the other end. "I like that. Okay 11 a.m. Wednesday it is. So, I will see you then. Okay?"

"Okay!" said Janet. "Unless I get abducted by aliens, I will see you then. Um, bye."

"Aliens, okay. Really hope that doesn't happen to you. See you—bye," and with that David hung up his phone on the other end.

Janet pushed the end call button on her cell. Oh my god, what have I just done? Janet thought and then she smacked herself in the forehead and leaned back in her chair. Well, coffee with a stranger, in a public location, only to talk business, and then to talk about the robbery. After that, a quick goodbye and she would return home. There isn't anything wrong with that. People do that kind of thing all the time. She just wished she could be one of those people, where social outings were a normal and easy part of life. That would be a nice change.

CHAPTER 3

All day Tuesday, Janet thought about her coffee meeting with the David guy. She should tell Eddie. No—he would just get jealous and make her feel bad and then she wouldn't go. It was just coffee, for Christ's sake. Not like she was having his babies or anything. In the end, though, she decided not to tell Eddie. Janet sighed, thinking her life would be easier if she could just have one without feeling as if she had to ask permission first.

Wednesday morning came and Janet overslept—well, woke up later than usual at 9 a.m. Janet liked to have a little mental down time before venturing out in the world, so as to kind of decompress before the stress, so she felt rushed. She took a quick shower and then, of course, spent an inordinate amount of time staring at her closet before saying out loud, "Just wear jeans, Janet! It's no big deal."

Janet grabbed the jeans she had been wearing yesterday from the pile where they were still sitting and slipped them on. Then she picked out a dark gray sweater to wear and pulled on some semi-dressy boots with 2-inch heels. She knew it was weird, but somehow wearing boots made her feel more in control. Which was problematic in summer, but that was a different story.

Janet grabbed her purse from where she always left it, unplugged her phone and stuffed it into her purse, and then put on a light jacket before walking upstairs to tell her kids (actually one kid and one adult) that she was going out to run some errands. This was technically true, since she planned on grabbing some milk on the way back from the coffee meeting. They really didn't need to know (or probably care to know) the rest. They both barely looked up from what they were each doing for a quick "bye." Usual response. Janet headed back down the steps and headed out the door.

Pulling into the Starbucks, Janet started getting butterflies in her stomach. Finding a parking spot far enough away that she would have to walk a little, she pulled her car into it and said to herself, "Okay, Janet." She took a deep breath, put her car in park, set the emergency brake, and took the keys out of the ignition. "This is not a date, this is just coffee. You aren't doing anything bad." After a little self-reaffirmation, she pulled down the car visor and took a quick glance at herself in the mirror. She hoped that the David guy wasn't watching. It would be just a little bit embarrassing and weird to be seen primping.

Janet opened the door to the coffee shop and a blast of hot air instantly warmed her. The rich smell of coffee filled the air; it smelled so good she almost felt like she could taste it. Too bad coffee hardly ever tasted as good as it smells. Janet stopped for a moment and let her eyes slowly search the room. Okay, so where is he?

"There you are. I wasn't sure you would come," a man's voice said from behind her. Janet turned around quickly and found herself looking up at what she guessed was David's face. "See, not an axe murderer or anything—no axe." He held his hands up in the air, as if to prove the point.

Janet laughed nervously and then stuck out her hand. "Hi, I'm Janet," she said, which was the only thing her brain could think to say at the moment.

"Well, hello, Janet. I'm David. It is so nice to finally meet you. Okay, so would you like to order some coffee before we sit down? Remember, I'm buying."

"Sounds great," Janet said casually, smiling. Mmmm… everything smells so good. I feel like I could just eat the calories out of the air."

David laughed at that. "But wouldn't air food have zero calories? So you can eat as much air food as you want." David smiled and turned his attention to the menu board. "So what are you going to get?"

Janet turned her head so she could look at the menu board. Everyone around her seemed to spout out their orders without a second's hesitation… the ordering of coffee drinks anymore was like a different language all its own. "I think some chai tea sounds good."

"Sounds good to me too," David said, and turned to the barista. "Two grande chai teas, just regular would be fine." The person at the counter nodded cheerfully and got to work. David turned back to Janet.

"Why don't you find us a table? I'll stay here and get our drinks. Seems like it's getting pretty crowded in here, so we better jump on one fast."

"Yes sir," Janet said and then she laughed. Turning toward the restaurant, Janet quickly spotted a booth that two people were vacating near the front window, and she made a beeline for it before someone else could snatch it up.

"All yours," said one of the two women who were leaving the table. Janet smiled.

"But I didn't get you anything," she replied. The women laughed at her lame remark, and when they had finally gathered their things, they headed toward the door. Settling in, Janet took off her jacket and slipped into the booth, putting her purse next to her for safekeeping. She glanced back to where David was still standing. He was across the room, smiling at and talking to another person who was also in line. He seems really friendly and nice, Janet thought to herself. I need to quit being so paranoid.

After a few minutes, David finally joined Janet at the booth, sat on the bench across from her, and slid a hot cup of chai tea toward her. Janet grabbed the cup from the center of the table and carefully slid it across to her side.

While David was taking off his coat, Janet took a quick look at him. He had brown hair; brown eyes... nothing special there. He was wearing a plaid button-down shirt and Janet guessed probably jeans, although she couldn't see them at the moment. Janet was glad she had picked the casual outfit she had worn; she hadn't wanted to seem overdressed. David, at least for this meeting, seemed to pick clothes for comfort rather than for fashion, and Janet could see absolutely nothing wrong with someone doing that.

"So, what do you want to talk about first... the robbery or my house?" David took a quick sip of chai and then looked up at Janet.

"Hmmm. I think I want to talk about the robbery first. Isn't that the craziest thing? You always hear about these things on TV and you think they will never happen to you and—there it is. Well, it didn't really happen to me, but I kind of feel like I dodged a bullet." Janet took a sip of the tea and closed her eyes in enjoyment. "Love this stuff."

"Okay, the 'bank heist' it is."

David started to fill her in on all the details of the ordeal. How two men waving guns around pushed into the bank and yelled "Everybody down to the floor!" In the surprise and confusion, people started getting down onto the floor, but one guy seemed a little too slow for one of the robbers' liking. "Down," he had said, shifting the gun so it was pointing directly at the guy's face. The bank customer's eyes got wide and he had then moved quickly to the floor, joining the others who had already done so.

"Face down, on your stomachs everyone. And put your hands on the back of your heads. I want to be able to see those hands. Don't want any of you texting your dad or something. And you guys, behind the counter... don't touch anything or I will shoot you. Come on out here and lie down with your customers. Remember, customers always come first." The robber had kind of laughed at himself with that one but then his face had turned serious again. He pointed his gun at one of the people from behind the counter. "Except for you."

David then told Janet how the robbers had gotten as much money as they could from the bank drawers; when that was done, they had politely asked the bank customers to pull out any money they had out of their purses or pockets, because, the one had said, "I would hate to check your pockets and find out you thought you could get away with something." The bank customers complied. After grabbing their bags, one of the robbers had said, "Have a nice day," and then they had both run out of the bank.

"They didn't say, 'have a nice day,' did they? That is too funny," laughed Janet. David had a great way of telling a story, using different voices for the different people. He talked as though he were drawing a picture with words.

"I swear to god," David said. "There must be books out there published online that are called 'How to Rob a Bank Nicely'."

Janet laughed, "Or 'Proper Etiquette for the Perfect Heist'." They both laughed at that and then took sips from their tea.

"Gee, I'm so sorry I missed it…. Not. Really don't need those images going through my head. Oh, and thank you. Now I do have those images going through my head," Janet teased.

David laughed. "You are a funny one. So, I guess we can talk about my house now? Or do you have any more questions you want me to answer about the robbers, maybe describe what they were wearing? Or about how I bruised my knee because I got down to the floor so fast?"

Janet covered her ears and laughed again. "No, I think I've heard enough. We need to change the subject or I won't be able to sleep tonight. Yes, please…tell me about your house."

David smiled. "Okay, about the house then." David started to fill Janet in on his house, how he had gotten a home equity loan, and then the loan crisis happened and now he was behind on his mortgage. Janet listened intently for a few moments and then asked, "Have you been out of work?"

David frowned a little and then quickly said "Um, no. About 2 months ago, my wife and I separated. It was pretty ugly. No kids, but a lot of anger on both sides. She still won't sign the divorce papers and hasn't been keeping up with her part of the mortgage payment. I mean, she doesn't even live there anymore. She moved out long ago and I heard she had a new boyfriend she's living with. She is just plain crazy. I wish she would just sign the papers so I could be done with her. Sorry, maybe too much information."

"Oh, no. No big deal. I hear stories like yours all the time. Some much worse—you wouldn't believe what someone who once loved you can put you through. The stories…. Anyway, trust me, I won't tell a soul." Janet reached out, gave David a reassuring pat on his hand, and then realizing what she had just done, quickly pulled her hand away.

"I think you are just going to have to let your house go. Move on, start a new life. Sounds like you need a fresh start. I probably wouldn't want to take on your house sale even if I were still a real estate agent, honestly. I hate getting in the middle of family things and divorce wars and short sales can become ugly. I used to work with a guy who has skin as thick as an elephant and he has actually helped a lot of people in your situation keep their house. Which I assume you don't want to do?"

David sighed. "No way, too many unhappy memories. It was our dream home, with a couple of acres and we hardly ever saw our neighbors, except for every now and then at the mailbox. Our house is off a rural road, so we thought we could raise a family there away from some of the violence that seems to be happening more and more in the world. But, I guess that dream is dead. Right now, I think I would be happy to just walk away from the house."

"I understand," Janet commiserated. "Divorce is tough. I've had friends and family who have gotten divorced; it is not a happy time for everyone involved. I'm sorry."

"Don't be sorry," David smiled. "Actually you've kind of cheered me up today. I have been down in the dumps lately. Um, do you want to see my house... give me an idea of what you think it's worth?"

Janet hesitated for a moment. He seemed like a nice guy, and it would be kind of fun to do a little mental redecorating without spending her own money. Instead she said, "I'm sorry. I don't feel comfortable going over to your house, pretending I am still a real estate agent. I barely know you, we just met and I really kind of don't want to get involved. Sorry?"

David laughed. "The sorry again. Hey, that's okay. I understand. It's probably not a good idea anyway. House is a mess, half-finished projects everywhere, and I wouldn't want you to feel uncomfortable. Can you give me the name and number of your short-sale shark"?

Janet laughed. "Well, he isn't so much a shark as a piranha. No, I think I would save the shark label for others in the business, people who are not nearly as nice. I don't have his number with me; I cleaned out my real estate phone list a while ago, and it is all but a memory. Why don't you give me your number and once I get home, I can call and give it to you then?"

"Sounds good to me," David said, standing up and zipping his coat. "Want me to take your trash?" Janet handed him her empty cup and, after a quick dig through her purse, found a piece of paper to write David's number down on.

"Thanks so much for meeting with me. I know you probably thought I was a flake or somebody trying to put the moves on you, but really I'm just looking for a friendly face and someone to talk to." David stuffed his hands in his pocket and looked at the floor.

For some reason, Janet just felt like hugging him. So she did. At the last moment, he brought his hands out of his pockets and hugged her back.

"Thanks again. Well I guess we should go. Walk you to your car?" David asked.

"Absolutely. Love it when people walk me to my car. I might get lost or something, and then what?"

David laughed at Janet's joke. "You are too funny," he said as they left the Starbucks and headed over to where Janet had parked her car. True to form, Janet had parked far away from the entrance and in this case, it really had been the only spot she could find.

"You have a lovely parking spot," laughed David as he walked between the dumpsters to get to her car. "Is this your Hyundai?"

"Sure is," Janet said, fishing out her keys. "I will call you back with that number as soon as I get home. Thanks for walking me to my car."

David smiled and said "No problem" and he had started to turn around to head back to his car when he suddenly stopped. "Okay…." he said.

"Okay…what?" Janet asked as she started to put on her seatbelt.

David slowly raised his arms in the air. "I think I have a gun jammed into my backbone."

"Oh, so you have a backbone now?" a voice from behind David queried. "Well, that is amazing. Because you certainly seemed like you didn't have one when we were married…. Oh that's right, we ARE still married. So, who's your little girlfriend?"

During this whole exchange, Janet just kind of sat there dumbfounded. "Um, okay… what is this… David?" she said as she finally managed to get words out of her mouth.

"I'm so sorry, Janet. This is my EX-wife or soon to be ex-wife, Kelly." At that, Kelly took the gun she had been holding tight against David's back and jabbed it in even harder.

"Ouch, Kelly, that really hurts… now stop it!" David started to turn around to try to talk to Kelly.

"Stop it? I'm not going to stop it. You can't tell me what to do ever again," Kelly said. She then grabbed a big handful of David's hair and yanked it as hard as she could. David didn't make a sound.

"Nice to meet you, Janet. So—you are the little whore who has been sleeping with my husband. Fucking sluts are all the same." While still standing behind David, Kelly moved over to one side so she could get a better look at Janet. "Huh. Better looking than the other one. Or is it the other 'ones,' David?"

Before Janet could get a word out, David said acidly to Kelly, "I only slept with that one woman. And that was only because you, I come to find out, have been sleeping with tons of other guys."

Kelly laughed so hard she snorted. "Oh sure. If that is what you tell yourself to get to sleep at night." She redirected her anger toward Janet. "Oh, and Miss Janet, just throw me the keys to your car and put your hands on the steering wheel where I can see them."

This cannot be happening, Janet thought. Her hands were shaking and she fumbled with the keys while pulling them out of the ignition and almost dropped them onto the floor, before throwing them to David's wife.

"Um, Kelly, is it? I just met David, your husband. I assure you I'm not sleeping with him. I'm very married."

"Really? 'Cuz that's what the last one said. I guess to some people, what the hell! David, get in the passenger side of the car," Kelly said, She pushed him ahead with the gun in one hand while the other pocketed the keys. "We are going to take a little trip down memory lane."

"Kelly. Stop. Please stop. I won't ask for a divorce. Just let Janet go and we can deal with this on our own. Please? Kelly?" David pleaded.

"Oh, 'please, Kelly, stop'," Kelly laughed derisively. "You know, I wanted to talk a long time ago, but you wouldn't. You were too busy, and you were such a whiney asshole. 'I have to go to work. I'm sorry we can't go see your folks this year.' Whine, whine, whine. David, just get in the fucking car! Oh, and don't think about running, asshole. Or I will shoot your little whore."

Kelly smirked and looked at Janet. "Oh poor Janet, David wants to protect you. Oh yeah, sure he does. Then, watch out bitch…. Because he will use you up and when he is done… dump you."

David scrambled around the front of the car and got into the passenger seat. "Kelly, come on. Just let us go. We won't tell anyone, will we Janet?" David said, looking toward Janet plaintively.

"Oh, hell no. I won't say a thing. This is your business… not mine. I have a husband and two kids at home who are expecting me to return any minute," Janet quickly blurted.

"Yeah, right," said Kelly. "You probably live in Hookerville with all the other sluts. Just shut up, both of you. Put your seat belts on, safety first. And then, Janet, I want *you* to start the car, pull out very slowly, and without drawing *any* unwanted attention, start heading south."

David and Janet quickly buckled up and Kelly tossed the keys hard into Janet's lap. "I bet you like it rough," Kelly laughed. She put the muzzle of the gun up next to Janet's ear. "We will see."

Janet stuck the keys in the ignition, somehow started the car, and cautiously pulled out of the parking lot. "Okay, so I go south. Where are we going?" Janet asked. Janet wished she hadn't asked. Stupid mouth.

"Well," said Kelly, "We are going to visit my lovely house. Oh excuse me, *our* lovely house, right, David?" David, who had been quiet until then, finally seemed to realize that Kelly was seriously going to do this, to kidnap them. She was going to take them by gun force to their house. His Kelly! What the hell had happened to her?

"Kelly, please, I want you to move back in with me. We can start again. This time, I will get it right. Please, Kelly? Kelly, are you listening?"

Kelly wasn't listening. She was fumbling around in her big purple purse that she carried with her. "I am so fucking sick of listening to you talk," Kelly said and with that, she pulled a Taser gun out of her purse, shoved it into David's side, and pulled the trigger.

David's body started moving uncontrollably—it almost seemed to have a mind of its own. Then, with a little screaming sound, his eyes rolled back in his head and he slumped unconscious, falling over toward the car window.

"Ahh... much better. Wow, these work great. Should have gotten one earlier. Would have saved me a hell of a lot of trouble," Kelly said as she checked David to make sure he was really out of it. "Wasn't that fun, Janet?"

Janet was stunned, absolutely horrified about what Kelly had done to David. Janet was stopped at an intersection. She had come to a red light when Kelly had "tasered" David, but now the light was green and people behind her were honking angrily.

"Okay, stupid, drive," Kelly said to Janet, holding up the Taser. "Unless you want me to try out my little "bug zapper" on you?"

Janet snapped out of the trance she was in and quickly stepped on the accelerator. The car jerked forward. They were heading south.

CHAPTER 4

They had been driving for what seemed like hours to Janet. Kelly had her going down every back road in the county. Were they even in the county anymore? They had crossed over the bridge that went over the canal so many times, Janet had no idea if she was north of it or south of it anymore. Plus, it was starting to get dark, which really was a nice addition to the ordeal. Janet hated driving in the dark.

Kelly, still in the back seat, was rustling in her bag again. "Well I suppose my lovely husband will be waking up soon. Wouldn't want that to happen, would we?" Janet glanced in the rear view mirror, trying to find out what was up. Kelly was filling up a syringe with liquid from a small bottle.

"Uh, what are you doing? I really hate needles. Please no needles." Janet pleaded to Kelly.

"Well, aren't you the stupidest thing to walk the Earth. Why would I give you a sedative when you are driving the car so nicely? Janet, I'm not a total idiot. This is for David." Kelly leaned forward and reached around the passenger seat, pulled down the side of David's jeans as much as she could, and roughly jabbed the needle into his hip. David didn't make a sound, but soon his breathing became much quieter.

Janet was shaking like a leaf. This is not happening, she thought. She was just having a bad dream because David had been talking about the bank robbery while they were at the Starbucks. Tomorrow she would wake up, kiss her husband and her kids, and tell them all about her horrible dream.

"Janet. Hey Janet! You awake still? We're almost there," Kelly said from the back seat. "Pretty soon we can get out of this stupid car and then we can all get comfy in David's and my little house," Kelly said, smiling.

"I'm okay, no really, I am okay. I'm fine, not sleepy at all. I'm driving. See? Turn signals and everything," Janet said in Kelly's direction.

"Oh my god, you are a smart ass! And I really do hate smart asses. Yes, Miss Janet, good Janet, good dog. As we pull up to this intersection, I want you to pull the car over, put it in park, and shut off the engine. Then, you will shut off the headlights."

This is some sort of cruel punishment, Janet thought. I should have told Eddie what I was doing today. Crap, crap, crap. Her hands trembled as she started to reach for her purse.

"I'll take that," Kelly said as she ripped the bag out of her hands. "Ooooh, JC Penney's. High-end white trash... who knew David had such good taste?" Kelly took Janet's purse and threw it down by David's feet. "Now, I want you to get out of the car, slowly, Princess. And then put your hands behind your back."

Janet slowly opened the door of the car and stepped out. Her legs were so shaky she stumbled and fell to the ground. Dirt road, thought Janet, okay, at least I know we are on a dirt road.

"Get up clumsy bitch!" Kelly said to Janet as she stepped out of the back door of the car, one hand still holding the gun. "Now, would you be nice and turn so you are facing away from me? Think you can handle that, cupcake?"

Janet slowly got up from the ground and turned around; her back was now toward Kelly. "What are you going to do? I don't have much money. But I can get you some. I have a great credit rating. I could take out a loan." Janet rambled on for a little bit more before she felt the gun pressing deep into her side, right into the sensitive kidney area.

"Money? You think I want fucking money? God, you are getting stupider and stupider by the minute. Just hold still and don't move, or I will pull the trigger and your family will see how many lives you will save by becoming an organ donor." Kelly pulled a black bandana out of her pocket and wrapped it around Janet's head, making sure that her eyes were completely covered. Then she pulled tight.

Janet just couldn't keep her mouth shut. "Owwww! You just pulled out my damn hair."

Kelly laughed. "Oh did I? I am so sorry. But I hear you can get hair extensions at Wal-Mart now, so don't fret." Kelly grabbed Janet by the shoulders and roughly pulled her closer to her. She then pulled a pair of handcuffs out of her bag and very indelicately put them on Janet's wrists.

"Oh, look you have baby wrists. Like a bird, looks like they would break in two like a twig if I even twisted one just a little bit." With that, Kelly twisted Janet's handcuffed hands roughly.

This time, Janet kept her mouth shut. She had to tightly push her lips together and fight hard to keep the words that wanted to come out inside, but she was able to remain silent. Kelly guided Janet slowly back to the car and helped her to get into the back seat.

"Watch your head. You can't afford to lose any more brains," Kelly said as she guarded the top of Janet's head with her hand. As Janet stooped and tried to get into the backseat, she misjudged the distance and fell in a heap on to the seat of the car. Kelly pulled Janet back up to a sitting position and strapped her tightly in, then shut the back door and opened the front. She started the car up and once again, they were on their way.

Janet was really scared, and in her troubled mind, she started to wonder if she would live to see her kids again. Thinking about Eddie and her kids, about how worried they probably would be by now about her, she silently wept.

CHAPTER 5

Kelly was quiet as she drove on through the night, which was good because it gave Janet some time to think. Okay, so no one knew where she was. Nobody knew anything about the person she had met up with that day. Her car, well... she was in her car... they wouldn't be able to find it, even. Oh my god, what the heck have I gotten myself into? Janet shifted a little bit in the seat and tried to relieve some of the pressure that the handcuffs were putting on her wrists. Wow, they really hurt. Janet thought, note to self: never get arrested. Oh, and never get into S&M and Bondage... or whatever acronym they called it... SMB? That didn't sound right. Janet held her breath and counted to 10 slowly, trying to focus on the situation she was in. She couldn't afford for her brain to be taking a trip to ADHD Land. Okay, I might already be crazy, Janet thought, but I think I am going crazier. I knew I should stay away far away from real estate. Real estate agents should get hazard pay for the risks they have to take all the time. Janet quieted her thoughts and listened carefully, she could still hear David's quiet breathing. Well, at least he could sleep, hah... oh so funny, Janet. She really wished she could.

"Staying comfortable back there, are you, Miss Janet? I think we are almost there. Oh, wait! There it is, my house that I used to live in with David! I guess I took the scenic route! It usually doesn't take so long to get here." Kelly slowed the car down and then brought it to a stop, put it into park, and turned off the ignition. "Home sweet home."

Janet didn't know whether to be relieved, or to be scared, or... I mean, who would know how to feel in that situation? How did this happen? Janet had played and replayed the day in her mind. Seemed like a nice day. The tea was good. We have a nice talk and he seems like a friendly guy. Then psycho soon-to-be ex-wife kidnaps her husband and me and then tases her husband. Oh, and then she also sedates him. Oh wait, she also put a gun to my head and blindfolded and handcuffed me. Wow, this has been a great day! Janet kind of laughed, but only inside her head, because outside her head the world was totally fucked up.

"Okay honey, we're home!" Kelly said as she got out of the car, walked back, and then opened the backseat door. "Okay, you can get out now. I hope you enjoyed the ride."

Janet struggled to push herself up and valiantly tried to get out of the car on her own. Who knew it would be so freaking hard to do this with handcuffs on? Janet once again couldn't stop her mouth. "It would really be much easier for me to get out of the car, Kelly, if I didn't have these stupid damn handcuffs on."

"Holy crap!" Kelly said as she punched Janet's arm. "You really have a smart mouth that doesn't know when it's time to stop. Wow. I guess pretty soon, with some good old fashioned learnin', you'll get over that." Kelly reached into the car and around Janet, grabbed her handcuffed hands, and then yanked her roughly out of the car. Janet fell to the ground hard.

"Ow! That hurt!" Janet cried, wishing she could take back the many sarcastic things she had said to Kelly. "Okay, I get it. I will be nice and compliant and a good girl if you will please not hurt me anymore. Okay, please.... Kelly?"

Kelly laughed. "You know, I have to say... you are kind of funny. Considering the situation. I bet that mouth has gotten you into trouble more times than you can count."

"Yep," Janet said. "Stupid mouth. It really has a mind of its own. I try to keep quiet, really. But I think my brain is infected with "smart-assed-ness." I always seem to say the wrong things at the wrong time in the wrong place to the wrong people. Did I cover everything wrong there? Hmmmm...." Janet was so nervous and scared she was babbling.

Kelly twisted Janet by the shoulders so she was now facing away from her and then became strangely quiet, which kind of scared Janet. Just a bit. But to her surprise, Kelly took the handcuffs off and then proceeded to take off the blindfold. Not that it helped Janet to see her surroundings much. It was dark, very dark. She listened and could hear crickets chirping all around her... I love crickets, she thought. Again, she had to remind herself, hello Janet, earth to Janet, stop listening to the crickets and pay attention.

As her eyes adjusted to the light, Janet thought she could make out a few shapes. She could see trees, and maybe a building of some sort. But just as she was starting to get her bearings, Kelly finally found her voice again.

"Okay, tweetie pie Janet. You are going to help me get my stupid husband out of the car. I kind of want to just get in and shove his ass out the door with my feet and let him fall on to the ground. But the Christian in me thinks, 'Oh Kelly, don't hurt your loving husband... Hah!' Kelly snorted and laughed at herself. "Move your ass, Janet, and help me or I will shoot you both and bury your bodies where no one will ever find you."

Janet quickly walked around the front of the car and opened the car door to where David was still sitting, silently knocked out and oblivious to what was going on around him. Janet decided, okay, if I have to do this crap, I am going to be the best damn crap-doer around.

Kelly knelt down and grabbed David's feet. She pulled them as hard as she could, straining to yank him just a little bit out of the car. But Kelly really wasn't so much bigger than Janet. At 5 feet 5 inches, Janet estimated that Kelly topped the scale at maybe 145 pounds.

"Ahh, need a little help here, princess," Kelly snidely said to Janet. "Unless you really want to find out what it feels like to be chopped into tiny bits." Kelly had pulled out her gun again during that speech and was holding the weapon up close to her own face. Then she weirdly started rubbing the gun softly up and down her cheek… like a kitten or something.

"Right Mr. Gun? Oh of course, Queen Kelly. I will do your bidding," Kelly said, using some weird ass voice for the gun that Janet couldn't even begin to describe. She was crazy. Kelly was an absolutely crazy chick and she had a gun. Awesome.

CHAPTER 6

It was a lot of hard work, but Kelly and Janet finally somehow got David out of the car and onto the ground. Who knew one person would be so hard to move? Maybe Kelly should have just pushed him out with her feet. Janet stopped to take a breath and then very carefully asked Kelly, "What now?"

Kelly looked equally as tired as Janet did, if not more. "Well, now, honey pie… did he call you honey pie? He used to call me that. Well, now, honey pie… we are going to drag my darling husband. Don't panic, little Janet, we are only going to drag him for a short way. Would hate to see you cry some more and make more of a mess of that makeup of yours than you already have. Grab his feet."

Janet did as she was told. She leaned down and grabbed David's feet, finally deciding the best way to hold on was around his ankles. He was wearing some kind of hiking/walking hybrid…. Sketchers? Aren't those for kids? Weird. Janet shook her head and once again tried to focus. She looked out into the dark, toward where she thought Kelly was now standing, and found that she could kind of see a faint outline now that her eyes were beginning to adjust to the dark. Janet patiently waited for further directions.

"Okay, Janet. I'm going to be hauling the top half of this piece of crap and you are going to be holding the feet end of this piece of crap and we are going to start moving forward."

Forward, what was forward? Janet thought. Kelly grunted and somewhat lifted part of David's head and torso off the ground and started dragging him in the direction that was apparently "forward." Janet held on to David's ankles and tried her best to help move his sleeping body to wherever they were headed in the dark.

It was hard going. There was a slight slope to the ground and before long, Kelly was breathing hard. She stopped to cough, and then unceremoniously dropped David's body and head to the ground.

"David, you could stand to lose a few pounds. How are you doing back there, Janet?"

Janet stopped and dropped David's feet. What? No stupid? No whore? No cupcake? Just Janet? Janet didn't know what to do with that. "I'm okay," she said, hoping all this hard work was taking some of Kelly's anger away.

But the old Kelly was already back. "Okay, Little Miss Pussy, only a couple more feet and we will be at your new house. I think you will love it."

My new house? thought Janet to herself. Oh Jesus. Crazy lady had brought me into some weird-ass psycho world of hers that she was living in. Okay. Janet, be quiet and listen, Janet reminded herself. Hadn't that been what her Mom had always told her? Thinking more about her Mother, who was in a coffin in Montana, Janet suddenly felt tears start to well up in her eyes. Her Mom had been tough. Janet remembered her Mom's stories of growing up with an alcoholic mother who didn't pay much attention to her, which had forced Janet's Mom to grow up too fast.

Kelly's loud voice broke her reverie and brought her quickly back to the present. "Okay, miss leg spreader, we are going to stop right about... here," Kelly said and once again dropped David to the ground. At least this time his head didn't hit the hard dirt. This time, as it hit the ground, his head sunk into some tall grass.

Janet dropped David's feet, or whatever, she was so tired she didn't care if she was carrying an atomic bomb or baked Alaska… she could not carry David another step. Gasping for breath, Janet silently waited for what Kelly had to say.

Kelly was equally, if not more, out of breath and seemed to be hurting from the exertion. Janet wondered if maybe Kelly had underestimated how hard it would be to drag her husband. The car seemed an awfully long way away from where they were now. It was obvious that Kelly had planned this. She probably had been planning this or some version of this for a long time. The gun, the Taser, the syringe, the blindfold, and the cuffs… Kelly was one really pissed-off lady. Was she insane? Had she always been insane? Why would David, who seemed so nice and kind, marry someone who swore like a truck driver and clearly exhibited signs of someone who was definitely not quite right in the head?

A loud crashing noise from something nearby made Janet jump, startling her back to the present. In the pitch-black darkness, Kelly had obviously picked up and then heavily dropped something hard to the ground.

"Okay, Janet. Here's the fun part. We are going to push David … and he is going to fall… don't worry… just a little ways … into your new home. Isn't that exciting, Janet? Maybe you could get some pretty curtains and a throw rug to brighten up the place."

Janet felt every hair on the back of her neck stand on end. Oh my god, Kelly is going to lock us in some underground dungeon and ooooh… shit! I just know there will be spiders. Lots and lots of them. And gross crawly things that want to live in your ear and make babies and then dig their way out through your brain.

"Kelly. I understand you are really mad at your husband. And I would be too," Janet quickly added. "But… you seem like you are a really sensible and intelligent person. You aren't really going to put us into a hole in the ground?"

Kelly laughed. "Oh, Janet! I might be mad, but I'm not a sicko. It isn't just a hole in the ground. Think of it as a little underground apartment love nest—a present for your honeymoon. Won't it be romantic, just the two of you?"

Janet wished, just wished she had somehow magically suddenly gained some psychic powers. Then she could summon Eddie or the police with her thoughts alone, they would come and rescue her and David, and this would all be over. Janet knew there was no way she was going to go down willingly into that hole in the ground. So, without thinking, Janet ran.

Where she was going, Janet had no idea. She figured Kelly would have just as hard a time seeing in the dark as she did, so Janet thought she might just have a chance to get away. But Kelly had obviously thought ahead. Out of the purple purse came the night vision goggles. Kelly quickly slipped them on her head and started running, gaining fast on Janet, who was trying her best not to trip over crap in the dark. Janet could just picture herself tripping over something, hitting her head on a rock, and then... goodbye Janet.

"Janet!" Kelly yelled. "Sweetheart. You aren't going to get away. I can see you."

Crap. Judging by the loudness of her voice, Kelly was much closer than Janet thought she was. *Play dead*, Janet thought. That is what they always told you to do with bears. So she did. She quietly lay down on the ground and tried desperately to control her breathing so Kelly wouldn't hear her and find her.

But Kelly did anyway.

"Hey. Sleeping Beauty. Get up. Prince Charming is waiting for you back at your new love shack and I would hate to have to tell him that his favorite whore... um, gee, sorry... has a hole in her head."

Crap! Janet thought. Why couldn't she get a break? Oh wait, this is always the way it happens in movies. The hot chick (that was her) tried to get away and the evil monster (that was Kelly) let the hot chick think she was getting away... but the hot chick never did. The monster always re-caught her. Janet picked herself up slowly from the ground and tried the best she could to get some of the dirt off of her hands and knees.

"I'm so sorry Kelly. I panicked. I stupidly thought you were going to put me in a dirt hole. But, I know you wouldn't do that, so I'm very sorry to have run away." Janet was trying to think as fast as she could, which at this point wasn't very fast. She was stressed, tired, and hungry and scared for her life.

"Janet, baby. It's okay. I would have done the same thing. Come on, let's go back to where David is waiting, and both of you together can have a little rest and relaxation. You clearly need it. I can tell." Kelly was talking in a weird and creepy voice again, which scared Janet even more than the yelling did.

Janet followed Kelly's lead (or actually, Janet led the way because Kelly had the gun rammed into her back), and they walked until they were back where they had started. This was not going well.

Clunk! Janet thought she would never get that sound out of her head. Where had she heard that before? Oh yes, the post office. Funny, it sounded just a little more strangely hard and at the same time hollow when a human body hit the ground from maybe… seven feet? Janet didn't know. She wasn't a mathematician… or a physicist. And really, who cared how many feet per second some almost-stranger had traveled before he hit the ground when she was soon going to end up down there with him.

"Awesome. In the hole. David is in the hole. Janet! Oh, Janet? You're next." Kelly grabbed Janet's arm and roughly pulled her toward the hole. "Oh, don't worry Janet. I'm a nice person, really. There's a ladder. You can just scurry on down and soon enough you will be reunited with your honey."

Kelly guided Janet over to the hole and helped her put her foot on the first step of the ladder going down. "See? Nice sturdy ladder. I'm nice to you, aren't I?"

Janet said nothing. She was petrified, afraid to say yes or no for fear of what might happen to her next with either answer.

Slowly Janet climbed down the ladder and much to her surprise, stepped off onto a concrete floor.

"See, I'm nice. Too bad David didn't see that, the asshole. But he'll learn. There are always consequences to your actions; you can't escape what you did to hurt other people. David should have known that. And I'm sorry. Janet. He played you, too." As Janet watched in the dark, Kelly slowly pulled the ladder up and out of the room and the square door overhead came crashing down... blocking out the little light that there had been from the night sky. Janet couldn't see a thing. She was scared out of her mind.

CHAPTER 7

Crickets, I can still hear crickets. That's good, right? At least the sound of the crickets helped her know in her head that she hadn't exited the world. Janet hugged her arms around herself, trying to stop the shakes that were slowly moving through her body. After a few minutes of doing breathing exercises (hey, Lamaze comes in handy, she thought) and counting sheep and imagining a shiny bright crystal, or whatever... she thought she had better check on David.

Poor David. Can you imagine being married to that woman? What the hell was he thinking? Was he crazy too? Or did he like the abuse? Janet had a million ideas and thoughts swirling around in her brain. After a quick search of the floor, blindly patting on the flat surface every couple of inches with her hands and arms extended, her hand finally found some sort of fabric. She had found where David had landed. I hope it is David, she thought.

She pulled herself toward him, and after figuring out head from feet (crap, it was dark in here) she slowly put her ear to David's chest and listened. Janet was glad to hear a reassuring "thump, thump" from his heart, and his body seemed fairly warm. How badly was he injured, if at all? Who knew? Janet was just glad to finally be able to grab on to something that seemed real and in this world and not just the craziness and thoughts that flitted through her mind. She kept her ear and her head down on David's chest and before she knew what hit her, she fell into a deep sleep.

EEEEEK... clunk! Janet awoke to an awful creaking noise, located somewhere in the space way above her head.

"Breakfast time," she heard a loud voice say. Janet's memories of the previous day quickly returned. Oh yeah... it was sweet and lovely Kelly, David's crazy kidnapper wife, screaming from above. Janet had barely a chance to open her eyes when what seemed to be a huge bunch of boxes and bottles and stuff rained down around her body. After she thought the pelting might be over, Janet rubbed her eyes and tried to look up toward the bright sunlight that had filled the trap door, shining impossibly bright. The sun—had it been that long since she had seen it?—seemed so bright now it seemed to burn through her eyes. She couldn't look at it for more than a second before she quickly had to shade her eyes as much as she could while still trying to see something, anything that might connect her to the outside world.

"Awesome, thanks! Room service, what a treat," Janet grumbled, just loud enough so she knew Kelly would not miss her comment. Janet, cold, tired, and angry, could definitely not stop her mouth from the oozing sarcasm that wanted to spill out and drown the world. Who cares now, she thought to herself, what the fuck? She was already underground in a dungeon, trapped by a crazy lady who talked to her gun, and who was convinced that Janet, who had just met the guy, was "doing it" with her man.

"Don't be snotty. You don't need to be snotty," Kelly replied sourly, and then she shifted her body in a way that made the light that was entering in to Janet's darkness seem even more blindingly bright. Janet closed her eyes; she could still see the sun burnt into her retinas even though her eyes were closed.

"I'm sorry. I appreciate the food. Which I think this is, isn't it?" Janet tried to soothe her, the lady who was now her only contact with the outside world, and really the only person, as far as she could tell, who could set her free. Maybe Kelly was a different person today? Maybe after a night of sleep, she had a change of heart and would let Janet go. Who knew with crazy people?

"Why didn't you turn on the lights? Oh, that's right... you are stupid. Any idiot would think, 'Gee, there might be lights,' and look to find them. I guess you haven't even risen to the level of idiot yet. Poor Janet."

Janet was livid. She bit her lips hard, and somehow resisted the urge to scream profanities and/or hurl random crap at that crazy woman. But she thought better of it and as her eyes adjusted, she took a quick look around and finally spotted a light switch. Thank god. Now the spiders won't get me, Janet hoped.

Kelly, hearing no reply, yelled down into the hole, "Okay, then. Why don't you eat your breakfast and maybe, if I haven't given Mr. Stupid Man way too much medicine, your darling David will wake up and you can share your happiness with him at being in your new love nest together. I'll be back later. Or not. I haven't decided," Kelly laughed. Janet watched helplessly as the trapdoor was slowly lowered and the space again descended into total blindness.

Trying to get her bearings, Janet's most urgent need was to find that light switch. First, she started swishing her hand around in the space near the ground next to her. She didn't want to trip or run into something. Her hand first felt and then hit something solid... a small box? She held it up close to her head and shook it. Corn? She smelled the box and then her childhood brain remembered what she smelled. "Oh, drat. Corn flakes. And I was hoping for the breakfast of champions." Janet continued across the room, sweeping her hands back and forth in front of her face until she had crawled over—it really wasn't that far—and reached a wall.

Yes! Janet thought. She slowly stood up, and with that movement, she quickly felt a little unsteady on her feet. Groping around in the dark for a few seconds, Janet found the light switch. Breathing a sigh of relief, Janet flipped the switch and the room was, by quick steps, slowly flooded with lights, really big old blinding lights. Janet again shaded her eyes. Large old-fashioned rectangle fluorescents hung from the ceiling and fully filled the room with a clear blue light. Oh thank god, Janet said to herself. Ever since she was little she had hated being in the dark. As the fluorescents finally flickered to their full capacity, Janet felt her mood brightening along with the increasing brightness of the light around her.

Looking around the small room, Janet started to begin to assess her situation. Before she could figure out what was what in the space, she heard a quiet groaning from across the room. It was David.

"Ahhh yuck... oh my god, I feel like puking. What the hell? Where am I? What the fuck?" David said in a stream of words... right before he threw up all over the floor. After a minute or so of vomiting and then some final spitting, David finally seemed like he didn't have anything left in him. He wiped his mouth with his sleeve, squinted his eyes as if light was a new experience for him too, and looked around the room. After a few seconds of that, (there was hardly anything to look at), David said, "Okay, seriously. Where the fuck am I?"

"Oh, I'm sorry. That's right, you missed the fun car ride that I took you on yesterday. It was so fun and scenic, so many lovely sights and beautiful vistas... I wish I had a camera with me to share everything with you... and wow, I just love getting a gun pointed at me. Great day!" Janet said as she stood there looking at David who now, quite hopelessly, was trying to get up.

After a few tries, David gave up and sat back down on the floor, trying to get his bearings. He seemed at first to have no recollection of what had happened, and then... "Oh god. Now I remember. Kelly. What has she gone and done to us? Wow, I sure can pick them, can't I?" David looked around the room, an action that was soon interrupted by a coughing fit. "I need something to drink. Is there anything?"

"Oh just a minute, I will check the mini bar. Are you crazy? Look around; this isn't the Hilton in Chicago or something. I don't know, I just found the light switch. That has pretty much been the highlight of my day so far." Janet took a quick glance around the room and spied a water bottle that had landed and then rolled underneath a shelf. "Ooh, we are in luck. Water. Here," Janet said as she scooped up the bottle and threw it to David.

Not expecting something to be thrown his way, David flinched and rather than catching the bottle, put his hands up to protect his face. The bottle fell to the ground and rolled a short distance away. After a second or two, realizing that nothing else was going to come sailing in his direction, David reached for the bottle, opened the lid, and took a long drink.

"Whoa! Don't drink it all. I don't think there is a 7-Eleven down here anywhere close. That might be the only water we get to drink for a while." At this, Janet started to look around the room, trying to find the other things that had pelted down on her from above. After a few seconds of searching—it wasn't a big room after all—she found two mini-boxes of corn flakes, another water bottle, and a roll of toilet paper.

"Well good news and bad news. We have another bottle of water, we have corn flakes, and we have a roll of toilet paper. I'm thinking the toilet paper is one of those kinds of good news/bad news kind of things. Like, 'yeah, we get toilet paper' and then 'boo, um… where is the toilet?'"

Janet, not knowing what else to do with it, put the toilet paper roll on a rickety homemade shelf that stood against the wall, the only other thing in the room, and then walked over to where David was sitting and handed him one of the boxes of corn flakes.

"Thanks," he said, grabbing the corn flakes. He quickly ripped open the box and started to eat the cereal by handfuls. "Of course, no milk."

"Well, at least it's something. If you don't mind, I'm going to sit over there," Janet said pointing to the wall furthest away from David. "Not to hurt your feelings or anything, but it kind of smells a little vomit-y over here." Janet walked over to the wall she had pointed to, leaned against it, and then slid her body down until she was sitting on the floor. She opened the bottle of water, and started to drink… she hadn't realized how really thirsty she was, but at least she had the sense to stop herself from drinking too much of it. Who knew how long until they would get more water, or if any? Janet then opened the box of corn flakes… they smelled so good and tasted much better than she remembered them tasting. Janet dug into them. Holy cow, she was hungry. The last time she had eaten was yesterday morning at home. Yogurt, she remembered. Crap, Janet thought to herself, I should have splurged on the calories and gone for a big old fat muffin yesterday at the Starbucks. But… who in their wildest dreams would think that she would end up in this unbelievably crazy situation? Janet soon finished off her corn flakes, put the small box down on the floor, and turned her attention back to David.

"So, how were those corn flakes? Best ever, huh," Janet remarked. "Sarcasm, the breakfast of champions."

David, who had apparently already eaten his box of corn flakes, was checking out the bumps and bruises on his body, bruises he didn't at all remember getting. His whole right side felt like one giant bruise and his head had definitely run into something hard. "Okay, I hurt. So, I'm guessing I was knocked out? For how long?"

Janet stretched her legs and started massaging her calves, trying to coax some of the stress out of her body. "Let's see, you got tasered in the parking lot at the Starbucks, and then on the lovely and long road trip Kelly kindly gave you a shot of some sedative or sleeping thing or something. Oh, and by the way, your wife? She has issues. She really rammed that sedative needle into your butt."

"Ahhh, that explains the butt pain. Kelly is a registered nurse. I think she must have done a little hospital pharmacy raid or something, stocking up for her planned crazy vacation." David reached down and started untying his shoes. "My feet are killing me. I hate sleeping in my shoes."

"Yeah, such a bother, all that sleeping… and the oh-so-constricting shoes. Wish that was all I remembered. So, let's see. The fun almost all happened yesterday. It's a brand new day, and a few minutes ago, your wife rained down corn flakes from heaven. So you were out, or as I am starting to think, 'blissfully sleeping,' I don't know, you do the math." Janet followed David's lead and unzipped her boots and slipped them off her feet and sighed. "Breathe little toes, breathe. I'm talking to my toes… just in case you wondered."

David kind of half-laughed at her remark. "Still funny. Down in a hole in the ground after being kidnapped by some virtual stranger's wife and you still are cracking jokes. Are you always so funny?"

"Oh absolutely," Janet said as she put her boots back on her feet. "I'm the life of the party, the class clown… or crass clown… I can't decide. Really, truly, I'm not really trying to be funny; I would just love to experience a normal person's reaction in any or all situations. But I am who I am. Which is unfortunately kind of off-putting to a lot of people, but it helps me cope. Lucky me."

David shook his head and laughed again. "Well, I admire you. Being able to make a joke in a freaking unbelievable situation like this. I'm glad that you have something inside you that helps you cope. As an added bonus, it makes me laugh. So, please, feel free to keep up the banter. I think we both could use a little levity at this particular moment in time."

"So, maybe you want to clean up a little bit of that barf?" Janet asked, hoping to change the conversation while at the same time hoping she could spend whatever time she had down here without have to plug her nose. "We have toilet paper to wipe it up with. It would be nice."

"Right on it, sorry." David, still a little slow, eventually understood the message, grabbed the toilet paper off the shelf, and proceeded to clean up the vomit. "Um, what should I do with this?" he asked, holding up the disgusting toilet paper.

"What? I don't know. Do I look like an authority on the subject? Try to stuff the crap into one of the corn flake boxes and then take it and put it in a corner. Far away from me." Janet got up off the floor and looked around. "Okay, now serious stuff. What is this, a storm shelter? A fallout shelter? What?"

David looked at her inquisitively. "Um, how should I know? I was knocked out when I got here, remember"?

Janet looked perplexed. "So you don't have anything like this near your house or anything? Because Kelly said she was taking us to your house."

"No, we don't have anything like this near our house. I think I would notice something like this little hidey hole." David looked around again and started going around the perimeter of the room, seeming to search for something while randomly touching the walls.

"Oh good," Janet said. "So… we really, really don't know where we are. Awesome. My day keeps getting better and better. What exactly are you doing, anyway?"

"I have no idea. Just looking at the walls, testing for cracks or hidden doors or just maybe a way to get the hell out of here. Want to help?" David asked.

"Well, I'm no engineer… but those walls look pretty damn solid to me. The only way I can see to get out of this place is up there through where we came in. But, there is electricity coming into this place. Where do the wires come in?" Janet scanned the overhead fluorescents trying to follow a logical route.

"Good idea. Okay, wait a second…. Wait a second…. Found it." David pointed to a spot about 6 inches above the floor. "That is where the electricity enters the room."

"Crap. How does that do us any good? Even if we somehow got through the wall, there would be a couple of tons of dirt to dig up through. Well, I guess we will keep it in mind. Maybe there will be some way we can use it."

Janet looked around in disappointment. Really, the only things in the room were four walls, a rickety wood shelf that looked like it had been made by an eight year old, the ceiling, the floor, the fluorescent lights, the trapdoor above, and ... a light switch. "Hey, maybe we can figure out something with this light switch. It's further up the wall. Maybe there is a way we can pry the electrical box out and work away at the cement from there."

"Yes, hmmmm. Let me take a look at it." David walked over to the light switch and wiggled the cover a little. "But what if we accidentally cut the wires and we end up with no light? That would be extremely sucky. Fuck!"

"Wahh!" Janet looked around and, seeing nothing, sunk back down on to the floor where she had been sitting before.

"So, how did I get in here? And better yet, how did you get in here?" David walked over and sat against the wall opposite from Janet.

"Well..." Janet began. "After I helped your lovely spouse drag your ass about, I don't know, 80 feet, she opened the hatch-door, and then we just pushed you in."

"Oh, nice. Wow thanks for that." Seeing Janet's scowling face, David added, "I know, you had to do what you were told to do. But how did you get down here?"

"I got to climb down a ladder, which your wife quickly took away. It was so freaking dark in here; I couldn't see anything but pure blackness. And it was cold. So, only to keep warm, mind you, I found where you had landed and then slept right next to you to keep us both warm. I slept like a rock. On a rock. And then later, the door in the ceiling opened up... and you know the rest." Janet put her hands up and ran her fingers through her hair. "I feel like I haven't showered in days."

David thought about what she had just said, and then asked, "So, you really have no idea where we are?"

"Nope," Janet sighed dejectedly. "She made me drive around for so long I didn't know which way was up or down. Then she made me stop the car, and she put handcuffs and a blindfold on me and stuffed me into the backseat. And then she drove around some more. Ooh, one thing I do know. We were stopped on a dirt road. And there was grass. I guess that is technically two things."

"So we've got dirt road and grass to go on." David rolled his eyes and exhaled. "I had no freaking idea Kelly was this crazy."

"How crazy did you think she was? Was she always like this? What did you do to piss her off so much? You don't think she is going to kill us, do you?" Janet started rambling off questions so fast David couldn't keep up.

"Whoa. One question at a time," David said. "And I'm going to try to answer them the best that I can in no particular order. No, Kelly wasn't always like this. She was so much fun when we first got married. She had just finished nursing school and I had earned my degree in engineering. We couldn't get enough of each other. We loved to hike and explore, go to movies, and eat at restaurants…everything just seemed perfect. But then it all started to change. Can't really pinpoint when, but Kelly became withdrawn. She didn't want to go out. She stopped seeing her friends. She put on about 20 pounds and…. she just changed, toward me, toward the world…. I don't know what happened."

Janet listened intently. "So, she mentioned something about somebody cheating? Was that on both sides, or just on one? You have no idea how uncomfortable I feel asking this question, but I think I need to know as much information about the situation as I can. And now I will shut up so you can answer."

A smile flashed on David's face and then quickly went away.

"Um, okay. I started to notice Kelly coming home a little later from the hospital than she usually did. She would say, 'Oh, I was helping another nurse clean up a mess,' or 'traffic was really bad,' or 'another nurse decided it was a good time to talk about her trip to Bermuda' and how she couldn't find a way to get away without seeming rude. Which was fine, I knew from the beginning that nurses worked long and difficult hours. Then she started calling from work saying she was 'going to pull another shift for another nurse' and that she wouldn't be home later.' I was kind of disappointed; I kind of felt like we were two ships who passed in the night. We never saw each other, we both worked hard at our jobs, and with her weird hours, it was hard to get together."

Janet nodded her head in agreement. "Yeah, I know what you mean. At first in a marriage, you are everything to each other and then later on you start to realize that little bits and pieces of your time together are being taken away by 'stuff.' Happened to me and Eddie too."

"See, that is what I thought it was. Until one night... or was it morning? I can't remember... I got a call from her. She had been in a fender bender; she was all right, it was the other person's fault, but the car would not be able to be driven. The frame of the car had been bent into one of the tires and well, she couldn't drive it until the frame was hammered out. Her hospital was about a 25- to 30-minute drive away, pretty much a straight shot into the city. I knew the area pretty well. I told her it would take me a few minutes—had to get on some clothes—and then I asked her where she wanted me to pick her up." David paused for a moment, looked a little sad, and then continued.

"She proceeded to give me an address that was in the opposite direction of the hospital. That was weird, so I asked her why she was way out there. She said, 'Oh I was giving another nurse a ride home and she lives down in that new development near Newark, the ones that look like Monopoly pieces.' I knew which development she was talking about; it was really way out of the way. Kelly hated to drive at night and I was surprised that she had volunteered to give the other nurse a ride."

"Oh, I hate to drive at night too." Janet chimed in. "Especially in the rain... all the streetlights and headlights... their reflections bounce off the puddles in the road and it is so distracting... sometimes you can't even tell if you are in a lane or not."

David smiled. "I'm not a big fan of driving in the rain either. But I have to say it beats driving in snow."

Both of them smiled at that. Weather was easy to talk about, it was normal... it was a shared experience. After a few seconds, David continued.

"So, I got dressed, jumped in my car and in about 15 minutes I was at the café she had holed up in. She didn't look hurt, thank God, but she did seem really shaken. I told her it was okay, it wasn't her fault. I was just glad she was okay, and that the insurance would pay for it. After a brief hug, we left the café and got into my car. As I turned the car around and drove toward home, I asked her how it had happened. She proceeded to tell me that some jerk cut her off in traffic. She was forced to dodge out of his way to miss him, and as a result, she ended up hitting an SUV that was parked along the side of the road.

"I was quiet most of the time with Kelly until we got close to home," David continued. "Then, I asked her about the nurse she had given a ride home to. Was she someone I knew, was she new, what was her name? Kelly started to get a little snappish, then. 'Her name is Bonnie, no you don't know her, and she started about 4 months ago,' she said. Then she added, 'Got any more questions you want to grill me with?'

"The responses she gave, and the way she said them, did not seem like the Kelly I knew. She rarely ever was angry or crabby... I'm sure you find that hard to believe..." David directed this statement toward Janet.

"Yeah, just a little," Janet replied and then quickly added, "She seemed more than just a little crabby yesterday... in fact just a tad past what could be labeled crabby?"

David nodded his head in agreement. "So, after that, I apologized to her, said I understood that she was stressed and I promised to quit quizzing her. And as we drove up to the house she said, 'I'm so tired. I'm going straight to bed.' And then she did. She undressed in the bathroom while I slipped off the clothes I had thrown on earlier in the bedroom and crawled in under the covers. She came to the bedroom a few minutes later, grabbed her nightgown, put it on, shut off the light, and climbed into bed. Not another peep out of her."

"Okay, I would be stressed after a car crash. Everything goes in slow motion and the sounds you hear just stay in your head forever. Been in two myself." Janet added.

David stood up and stretched. While Janet shifted in her spot on the floor, David started to walk around the room a little bit. Janet thought she saw a change in David's mood, like this was now really becoming painful for him to talk about. She kind of felt bad for having brought up the whole topic in the first place.

"I'm sorry," she said. "If you don't want to talk about this anymore, we don't have to."

David stopped his pacing and turned toward Janet. "No, you should know. I want you to know. So don't be sorry, okay?"

"Okay," Janet said. "You're just starting to seem like you don't want to talk about it."

"Well, I don't and I do. But don't worry about me, every day I'm learning how to cope a little better." David crossed the room back toward where he had sat before and then slowly lowered himself to the floor until he was sitting. Janet could tell from watching David do that simple movement that he was really hurting from the fall. I am so surprised he didn't break something, Janet thought to herself.

"Okay. So it is the next day. I leave for work while Kelly is still asleep and start my day. It was about 2:30 in the afternoon when Kelly called and asked if I would drive her to work at 5 p.m. Earlier, she had talked to the repair shop; they had told her that her car wouldn't be fixed for a few days and that they were going to have to find a replacement part for the side that was smashed.

"I told Kelly, 'No problem,' and then asked her how she was feeling. She was a little curt with her answer to me. 'I'm fine; I just don't feel like talking on the phone right now. So,

I'll see you at around 4:30?' I agreed to make sure I was home early and she said a quick goodbye and hung up the phone.

"The day went by fast, as I had to hurriedly try to readjust my schedule to be able to leave work early. When I got home, I pulled in to the driveway almost exactly on time. The front door opened up, Kelly stepped out, turned around, locked the door, walked over with her head down, and then quickly got into the car. 'Thanks.' she said, while barely looking at me. I just smiled and touched her hand. I let it sit on hers for a few seconds, and then she pulled her hand out from under mine and then started digging in her purse for something.

"Realizing she still was bothered about last night, I started the car and headed toward the hospital. We got there just before 5 and Kelly said 'thanks,' grabbed her purse and her lunch, got out of the car, and quickly walked up to the building. She was strangely glancing around as if she were looking for somebody. But in a few minutes, she seemed to focus back in and remember her work schedule, and then she headed toward the door of the hospital.

"After I watched her enter the building, I started my car and began driving toward home. I hadn't gotten about 10 feet before my cell rang, so I stopped the car just a little way up the curb from where I had dropped Kelly off and answered my cell. It was my boss, Don. He wanted to know if I had dropped off the report he needed on his desk right away because he couldn't seem to find it. This is typical Don, so I started telling him exactly where I had put it. While I listened through the phone to Don thrashing around papers on his desk and waited for him to see the stuff he needed right in front of his nose, I happened to glance over toward the solarium that was part of the hospital's entranceway.

"Looking in one of the large windows, I saw Kelly standing there alone, and then suddenly a man I didn't recognize walked up to her, put his arms around her and gave her a hug, like he was just trying to comfort her or something. Then, to my utter amazement, this guy took a quick look around, and then he pulled her—my wife—off to the side of the room and started kissing her. I mean really kissing her, full body contact, hands wrapped around her waist, one moving toward her butt."

"Oh my god, what did you do then? I know what I would have done, and it wouldn't have been pretty." Janet shook her head in disbelief.

"Well, my first instinct was to jump out of the car, run into the hospital and beat the hell out of the guy for groping and kissing my wife. But about then, Don finally came back on the phone and started quizzing me nonstop about the report that he had finally found in his in-box, exactly where I had put it. I half listened to Don, while I watched the two of them, my wife and another man …and I'm sure in my amazement my mouth was hanging wide open. After what seemed to me like, I don't know, about five minutes, they separated. This guy then put his hand on the side of Kelly's head and he said something to her, and then they hugged again. After a few seconds of that, they broke apart, looked like they said goodbye, and went off in separate directions.

"I was flabbergasted. I could not freaking believe what I had just been looking at. In my head, I can still see the image of them kissing, with this guy's hand on my wife's ass… as if it just happened. It is burned into a part of my brain and I can't make that picture go away as much as I've wanted to and as hard as I've tried."

"Wow. Just wow" Janet said in disbelief. "What a nightmare vision that must have been. So what happened after that? When did you confront her"?

"Well, I didn't confront her at first. I just was so incredibly at a loss for words, I so had no idea what exactly I wanted to say, that I couldn't even approach her to tell her about what I had seen her do. So I just went home and went to bed, but of course, there was no sleeping for me. After Kelly's shift was over in the middle of the night and she had returned home, she came upstairs, quietly undressed, and slipped into our bed. I just lay quietly next to her and tried to pretend to sleep for the rest of the night.

"Kelly's next shift wasn't until 5 pm the next day. Sometime during the next day, the car dealer who was fixing her car had delivered a loaner car to our house for her to use until her car was fixed, so I didn't need to worry about driving her to work. But I left my job early that day anyway. I just couldn't focus. I needed to know more.

"I decided to go to the hospital directly after work and wait outside her building. I was going to wait until it was late at night, when her shift was finally over, and then watch and see what, if anything, would happen next. And then after that, do what? I don't know. It felt like I just needed to reconfirm to myself that what I thought I saw was indeed true: my wife was actually having an intimate relationship with another man. So I sat there in the dark car by the hospital, just staring out in to space, until late into the night when her shift was scheduled to be over.

"Kelly finally walked out of the hospital with another female nurse or doctor or something. They stood outside, in the dark next to the hospital, and laughed together at something one of them had said. After the conversation seemed to have come to an end, the other person waved and then walked off. Just as I thought I wasn't going to see anything else, all of a sudden a dark blue Chevy pulled up to the curb next to the hospital entrance. And I sat there, helpless, as Kelly walked up to the door of the car and got in, and the car drove away."

"Let me guess, you followed them," Janet said. She had been intently listening, following the entire sequence of events as David described them, and she very much wanted to hear the rest.

"Oh, hell, yeah. I followed them across town toward Newark to a kind of dumpy townhome community. They got out of the car, groped and kissed each other, and then walked to the door of the townhouse and went in. Wow, I had so much seen so way too much; there was no way I was going to wait around to see what happened next. I drove home. I was so mad and so hurt that I probably broke the land speed record, I was driving so fast. When I finally got home, I was broken. After finally going into the house and sitting on the couch, I started crying. I must have cried for an hour, probably longer. And then when I could cry no more, I lay down on the couch and fell to sleep. My brain had just shut down."

Janet had no idea what to say in response to David's story. He must have been devastated, seeing his wife like that. And then having to go home alone, and having to deal with his feelings, Janet imagined it was just too much.

"Wow," Janet finally said to David. "As hard as I try to, I can't tell you what I actually would have been feeling at that point. I just can't imagine the pain. I would hate that if I saw my husband kissing another woman."

"Yep, pretty hard to see. A while later, after a long, dark wait on the couch, I heard a key twisting in the lock and Kelly came in. She put her bag down on the table next to the door, flipped on the light switch, and then jumped when she saw me lying there on the couch. 'You scared the shit out of me,' she said, her eyes wide as she looked at the scene in the house. 'Why are you sleeping down here?'

"I paused for a few seconds and then, without any feeling or anger in my voice, just asked her straight out: 'Who is he?'

"Kelly stared at me for a second, looking like a deer in the headlights, the gears in her brain struggling vainly to keep up with what she had just heard and what she should say. With not enough time to think, she started rambling on and on. 'He? What do you mean *he*? There is no *he*. There is nothing going on. I don't know what you think you saw or what you think is going on, but he is just a friend, an orderly that works in the hospital and… David, really nothing happened. It was just a hug from a coworker who was concerned about the wreck I had gotten into and seeing that, you just must have misinterpreted it.'

"I just lay there on the couch, watching her scrambling for words and excuses. And I let her go on until I had heard enough and then I said, 'I followed you to his house tonight.

Nice neighborhood, by the way. I watched you walk into his house.'

"'I don't want to talk about this. You're crazy," Kelly said. She seemed extremely flustered and indignant with what I was saying to her, so much so that she stomped upstairs. After I lay there listening to a bunch of slamming around, things finally quieted down. She must have gone to bed. I was still lying on the couch. I hadn't even got up. I don't think my feet would have held me anyway. .... It is true, you know. Your heart can break. Mine did that night."

David's eyes started tearing up, he turned around, and Janet heard a sniffle and saw him wipe his eyes. She felt like jumping up and giving David a hug, but instead she decided to try to give David the space he so obviously needed. She just waited quietly.

David was like that for about a half an hour. Janet had walked around the room for a while, trying to stretch her legs and at the same time trying not to look at David. David was slowly becoming quiet and the crying had stopped. Janet wanted to say something, to comfort him somehow. Instead, she walked across the room to her spot by the wall and sat down to think. They needed to get out of here, sooner than later, or they would both go insane. Janet closed her eyes and before she knew it, she had drifted off to sleep.

CHAPTER 8

"I have to take a piss" was the first thing Janet heard David say. She had just woken up and her ears weren't quite awake yet enough to comprehend what he had just said.

"What did you say?" Janet yawned and stretched. She didn't think she had slept long, but she felt a little better... and her brain seemed a little fresher.

"I said, I have to take a piss." David was sitting on the floor across the room, near where the trapdoor was overhead.

"Okay. Well.... Why don't you just go to the bathroom? Oooh, that's right, we don't have a bathroom. Dang. And that would have been so easy." Janet was starting to feel like herself again. Her sense of humor had made a comeback.

David laughed, more than he had since this whole ordeal began. "Oh, you are funny. That is a gift. You should be a comedienne."

Janet laughed and then shook his head, "Really, *not* that funny. More just a tad bit too sarcastic. Gets me into trouble."

"Well, I think you're funny," David smiled again. "So going back to the somewhat urgent question, where do you think we should put the bathroom? I was thinking just off the Master Suite."

Janet snorted at that "Oh, now *you* are mister funny. I think we're going crazy, at an accelerated rate." Janet looked around, saw one of the now empty water bottles, and asked, "Have you ever peed into a water bottle before?"

"Um, actually no. I actually prefer to "pee" in a bathroom, like most civilized people," David quipped.

"Ha, ha! You used 'actually' two times in that sentence. Not good use of grammar." Janet really had no clue about what was good grammar and what was not; she just felt like trying to be funny, but not really succeeding.

"Yes, I believe I actually did," David said as he grabbed an empty water bottle and headed over to the corner where they had thrown the toilet paper with barf and the empty corn flakes boxes. "Now, no peeking."

"Trust me, I won't. I can even cover my ears if you want," Janet added.

David didn't reply and after a few seconds, Janet heard liquid start to fill the bottle. After David was done, he zipped up his pants, twisted the lid back on to the water bottle, and turned around. "If this was an Olympic sport, I would win gold. A nearly perfect score, barely even spilled a drop." David held the bottle up and then set it down into the "garbage" corner.

"Well, we are going to see how I do in the woman's marathon peeing event, coming up next." Janet picked up the other empty water bottle and looked at it. "I think this might be a little more difficult for me than it was for you. I haven't practiced much lately. Been so busy with the 10-city tour of my 'blowing of the nose' act."

"Well, after you," David said, and he gestured toward the newly designated pee corner. After they had traded spots, David sat on the floor with his back toward Janet. Janet just stood there for a second, stared at the bottle, rolled her eyes, sighed, then set the bottle down and started to pull down her jeans.

Janet had peed in the outdoors before. Who hadn't who had lived in the country? But usually it was behind a bush or a rock. Or it was dark. And she certainly had never had to try to "precision pee" into a bottle. Oh well, Janet thought, and took a quick glance at David to make sure he wasn't looking. She pulled down her pants and underwear, put the bottle down between her legs where she guessed the pee would go, and willed her body to pee. It took a few seconds before the pee came rushing out in a torrent. Janet's aim had been way off. She peed on her hand, she peed on her socks, and remarkably, she even peed a little into the bottle. But embarrassingly, Janet saw that most of it went on to the floor. Putting the nearly empty bottle down, she quickly reached over to grab the toilet paper, wishing she had moved it closer to where she was squatting, as she almost fell into the puddle trying to get it.

Janet tried to dry herself off as best she could. Even so, when she stood up and pulled up her undies and jeans, she felt somewhat like an idiot because she had peed on herself.

"Epic fail. Massive epic fail," Janet said in kind of a sports announcer type voice. "Oh, so sad for the Americans. She was the favorite to get the gold."

David laughed. "Are you done yet? Can I turn around?"

"Sure, turn around," Janet said to a laughing David. "You can even watch me clean up the giant pee lake I've made, that is, unless you want to help me."

David put his hands up and said "No, no. I will let you have all the fun. Be my guest. I'll just stay way over here and thank God I'm not a woman. Hah! Sometimes, I swear, they can be so helpless and stupid."

Janet wanted to say something to David about the "stupid" remark, but instead she chose to ignore it and just attributed the cutting remark to stress. Unrolling a bunch of toilet paper, Janet got to work cleaning up the urine puddle. Good fun, she thought to herself. After she was done, Janet desperately wished she could wash her hands. Obviously, that was impossible, so instead she sighed and tried to joke about her embarrassment to David.

"I peed on my socks. Don't know how I managed to miss my jeans, well—mostly managed to miss them, but I thank

God I did. But my socks… they are soaked, both of them. I really should have practiced more."

Janet walked a short way away, sat on the floor, and took off her boots. She pulled off her wet socks, and, looking around, she thought to herself that there weren't a lot of options for where to hang wet stuff down here. Since the rickety shelf was the only thing in the room, she hung them over the edge of it to dry.

"I guess I'll just let them dry here. I don't think anyone will steal them." Janet was trying so hard to be funny, but it was getting harder and harder.

David didn't laugh at her joke, or maybe, Janet thought, he just didn't hear it. She was about to repeat what she had said when all at once she heard the trapdoor above their heads opening. Even though they were in a lighted room, the sun still seemed blindingly bright to them. Janet and David both put their hands up to shield their eyes from the glare.

"Lunchtime!" Kelly yelled loudly down into the hole. "And if you don't want to get knocked unconscious by flying objects, I would suggest you both move your asses quickly away from the trapdoor vicinity."

Janet, remembering the raining down of corn flakes and water earlier, quickly scurried over to where David was standing. "Bombs away" Kelly said as she dropped two water bottles to the floor. The bottles each bounced once and then rolled a little ways before stopping. Next came two plastic-covered cartons. These kind of landed with a thud. With the impact, one of them tore open and what looked to be crackers spilled out of the box onto the concrete floor.

"Whoops, my bad," Kelly said. "But truthfully, they should make packaging more able to stand an impact. Like what? I don't know, maybe falling into a hole in the ground and hitting a concrete floor."

"Kelly, please, please let me out of here," David pleaded. Then realizing he hadn't said, "Let us out of here," David quickly looked Janet's way before he said, "At least let Janet out. She has family who is probably frantically worried about where she is."

Kelly scoffed. "Oh, now the big man is worrying about the family members and how they must be so worried. You know, you really are a fucking loser. Enjoy your lunch." And with that, Kelly swung the trapdoor back down into place and Janet and David were once again alone.

CHAPTER 9

The noise from the trapdoor falling was deafening. Janet stood there for a moment, covering her ears after the fact, as if that would help now. She should have covered her ears *before* the trapdoor fell. David had already headed toward where the food and water bottles had fallen and scooped up one of the water bottles and handed it over to Janet. Then he reached down, picked up one of the plastic-covered cartons, and turned it over in his hands.

"Yeah, Lunchables! I can't believe it. She gave us fucking Lunchables." After a brief inspection, David handed the intact package to Janet and gingerly picked up the torn one. Luckily, only some of the crackers had fallen out on to the cement floor. "Three-second rule. These are still good." David said and he reached down and grabbed a cracker from the floor, quickly popping it into his mouth. "Mmmm, floor dirt."

Janet laughed, opened her water bottle, and took a long drink. Then she made herself stop, put the lid tightly back on the bottle, and slid down to the floor with the water bottle in one hand and the Lunchables in the other.

"I don't think I've ever been this thirsty in my life. I feel like I could drink an entire lake." Janet looked down at the package handed to her. "Oooh, I got turkey and cheese with crackers… what did you get?"

David looked at his package while he was sitting down. "I got the same thing."

"Mine is better… it doesn't have floor dirt on it," Janet bragged.

"Well, mine is fortified with added minerals from the dirt on the floor, which probably makes mine healthier than yours," David said, adding, "Stupid over-processed food."

Janet had already started tearing into the turkey and was stuffing it into her mouth as fast as she could. The hell with making tiny sandwiches, she just wanted food. David was still eating his crackers.

Opening up his bottle of water, David stopped what he was doing for a moment and turned to Janet. "I'm sorry I got you into this mess. You seem like you're a very good person. You don't deserve this."

Janet finished what she was chewing and grabbed for a piece of cheese. "Well, I don't think you deserve this either. I'm not sure anyone deserves this… ummmm, good cheese. Amazing how anything tastes really good when you are starving."

David opened his water bottle and proceeded to drink it rapidly. He too sensed that he should conserve some of it, and when it was about two-thirds empty, he put the lid back on the bottle and set it on the floor.

"So, what would you be doing today if my crazy wife hadn't taken you on this lovely unexpected all-expenses-paid vacation?"

Janet thought for a little bit before answering. "Well, I don't know, because right now it is kind of hard to think about all of that, because then I will think of my family. My emotions are just running so high right now and I'm so stressed that I just can't allow myself to think about that. I really feel like I'm going to have a nervous breakdown." Janet stopped eating and set the package of food down on to the floor.

"I'm sorry. I should have thought. That was really stupid of me. Change of subject. What could we talk about? Are you enjoying the weather today?" David asked Janet, trying his best to be funny.

Janet appreciated his effort. "Well, it seems a little dry. But there is a chance of pee and maybe even some vomiting later in the day. So remember to bring your umbrellas." But Janet really wasn't in a joking mood now, and she pushed the rest of the food aside. "I think I will eat the rest of this later. My butt hurts, my back hurts, my head hurts, my legs hurt, and my feet are cold. I think the only thing on me that doesn't hurt is my hair." Janet reached up and patted at her head "Nope, that hurts too."

David nodded. "I feel like one giant bruise starting at my head and going down the entire side of my body. I can't believe I didn't break something from being pushed down into this hole like you said. I would not recommend that 'fall' to anyone."

Janet got up and did some leg and back stretches. She had never been an athlete or anything, but she had done some yoga classes and knew some things well enough to help her eventually get some of the kinks out. After a few minutes of stretching, Janet suddenly stopped. "Okay, fun is over. I want to go home. I just feel like screaming my brains out."

"Go ahead," said David. "Scream all you want. Maybe somebody will hear you and come rescue us from this hellhole."

"Okay, I think I will do a little screaming. You might want to cover your ears." After taking a few breaths to prepare herself, she let out a tentative but still somewhat loud yell. "Ahhhhhhhhhhhhhhhhhh!" she screamed, until she ran out of breath.

"Not bad," David said finishing up his lunch. "But I really think you can do better than that. Come on Janet, do it again, louder this time."

"Okay," Janet said, "you asked for it." Janet again took some deeps breaths and this time at the top of her lungs, she yelled, "Fuuuuuuuuuuuuuuuuuuck!" until nothing else could come out of her. "Better?" She asked, looking at David.

"Wow. You can scream. I would think anybody within a ten-mile radius would hear that. So how do you feel, any better?" David smiled and asked.

"Yeah, a little," Janet said as she sat back down on the ground. "Except now, for some strange reason, my throat kind of hurts." She reached over, picked up her water bottle, and allowed herself a little sip before quickly putting the lid back on.

"Okay, so Kelly cheated on you. I'm sure you were hurt and angry. But what did you do that made her so mad?" Janet asked. "If you are ready to talk about it."

"Well, I don't really want to talk about it but I think now would be as good of time as any to tell you. We have nothing else to do." David made a wry smile and started to tell Janet more of the story.

"Okay, so the next morning," began David, "I didn't go to work. I just couldn't move and I knew I didn't want to have to talk to people or to see people and then have to try to act like everything was normal. About the same time she usually gets up, Kelly made some noise upstairs doing whatever she does to get ready and when she was done, she quickly walked down the stairs. But seeing me there on the couch, her eyes got big, and she stopped at about the second step from the bottom. 'I was hoping you were at work,' she said quietly.

"'I'm sure you did,' I said. 'How long has it been going on? An orderly? You were fucking an orderly? Unbelievable.' Kelly slowly sat down on the step she had been standing on. 'I didn't mean for it to happen, I wasn't looking for it, but it just happened.' Kelly paused for a few seconds and then said quietly while looking at the ground, 'I am so sorry David. I know how hurt you must be.'

"'Hurt? Nahhh. I'm not hurt. Why would I be hurt by the fact that my wife is secretly fucking another man? Pissed off?

Now that, I definitely am. In fact, I am so incredibly mad at you right now, you just have no idea how really incredibly mad I am.'

"Kelly looked up and then looked at me, trying to think of something to say. 'It hasn't been going on long, only for a couple of weeks. We've only been together... in that way... a few times,' Kelly said, and then added, 'and we used protection.'

"'Well, thank god for that," I spat out at her. 'Thank you, thank you so much for that kind gesture. I just can't fucking believe this; you almost act like it was no big deal.'

"'Kevin and I didn't mean for this to happen.' Kelly again started to talk about the things she had done, trying to rationalize her behavior until I finally blew up.

"'Kevin? His name is Kevin? Kevin and I? You didn't mean for this to happen? Oh my god, Kelly. Do you hear the crap coming out of your mouth? Don't go into any details, please. I don't want to know, I don't ever want to know. I just want you to answer me one thing.' I looked squarely into my wife's eyes and asked, 'Is it over?'

"At that point, Kelly started crying. I mean really crying; she had lost it. 'Yes,' I heard her say between sobs. 'It is definitely over.'"

David turned to Janet, with tears in his eyes. "It was so hard to watch her cry like that, and not want to go over and put my arms around her. I mean she is my wife and I still loved her. I don't know, after that 'event' we kind of just went about our life, pretending nothing had happened. Things were really strained though. I dreaded coming home at night."

"So, you took her back? I don't know if I could. You must really love and care for her a lot." Janet had so much sympathy for David, he just looked so sad, that she reached over and patted his hands and then, realizing that she was maybe stepping out of bounds, put her hands back in her own lap. "So, what happened next?"

"Well, I hated coming home. So I started stopping at a bar on the way home. A couple of drinks seemed to make some of the hurt bearable. That went on for a couple of weeks, and eventually I started staying out later and drinking more. I was just trying to cope. One night, I got really hammered. I had gone to this one bar so many times that people there had started treating me like a regular. And of course, everyone wanted to drink shots that night. I knew I was drinking too much, but I didn't care.

I had just ordered myself another beer at the bar when I noticed a pretty blonde had walked up and was now standing right next to me. 'You got yourself a drink and you didn't get one for me?' she pouted. I knew she was hitting on me, and she was so cute, and so nice, and one thing led to another and I ended up having sex with her in my car in the parking lot. Afterwards I didn't really feel bad at all. It had made me feel more in control of my life, know what I mean?" David looked at Janet, waiting for her response.

"Um, I don't know. I don't know what I would do in that situation. I can't say." Janet looked uncomfortable and she fumbled for words.

David saw that he was making Janet uneasy so he looked away again. "After we did it, I asked if I could have her panties. I don't know why I asked, I just did. And strangely enough, she gave them to me. Wow, chicks are much different now than they used to be." David got up off of the floor and started to walk back and forth across the room.

"I was drunk and thinking about what Kelly had done, and some of the anger that I had built up inside was starting to pour out of me. Stupid and drunk, I drove my car home; luckily, I got there somehow without hurting anyone. I went into the house, walked up to our bedroom, dropped the panties on Kelly's head, and said, 'Damn, that chick fucked good.' And I walked away.

"Kelly woke up, turned on the light, and looked around the room. Once she saw what I had dropped on her head, she started screaming. Then she came running at me and started hitting and kicking me. I think she even bit me. She was just like a wild woman. I think she called me every dirty word in the book, and then some. And after she was done yelling at me, she walked to the closet, packed a bag, and left. She never came back to our house again."

"Wow, so that is what you did to make her so mad. Well, what the hell did she think you would do after she slept with this other guy? That you would just forgive her, things would be back to normal, and she could have her happy life back? I mean really, you only did back to her what she did to you. Well, pretty much, except for the panties part."

"Yeah, I think it was the panties that sent her over the edge. So since that time, the only way we've been in contact with each other, mostly, is through lawyers. She had pretty much moved her stuff and most of the furniture out of the house before the week was over."

"Why do you think she won't give you a divorce? It makes no sense to me. Wouldn't it be in her best interest, wouldn't you think? I mean then she could just get on with her life." Janet shook her head in amazement. "Sometimes I don't understand people at all."

"You and me both," David agreed. He paused for a few seconds before he finally added, "I know one of her grandmothers ended up in a mental hospital. I don't know if it was her Mom's Mom or her Dad's Mom. So, maybe that explains?"

"Sure helps explain why she is being such a psycho bitch. Craziness does run in families. Word to the wise, check their family trees for craziness before you get involved." Janet tried to joke about things, but she knew it wasn't a laughing matter. So she thought for a few seconds before adding, "Thank God Eddie and I have no mental illness in our family tree, at least as far as I know. Luckily, we only have heart attacks and cancer to worry about."

"You can always find something funny about a bad situation, can't you? Not in a bad way, but in a good way. You know how they say, 'Always look at the bright side of life?' You do that. I like that about you." David looked Janet straight in the eyes until Janet started to feel uncomfortable and looked away.

"Well, you are in a small minority of people who appreciate my humor and/or lack of. So thanks for the nice compliment." Janet smiled back at David and there was a moment or two of awkwardness.

"Well then, I don't know about you, but I feel like taking a nap. This sleeping on a hard cold floor really sucks. And it's hard to sleep with the lights on 24/7. Do you think we dare turn them off for a while so we can take a nap? Oh, I mean that is, if you are going to take a nap. Never mind, we will just keep the lights on." David sounded a little flustered. Janet couldn't help but think that was a little cute.

"No, I think that is an excellent idea, a nap. And yes, what the hell, let's turn the lights out for a while. I might sleep a little better."

"Then so it shall be," said David as he got up off the floor and stood next to the light switch. "Let me know when you're comfortable and I'll turn off the light. But after that, please do not move. I don't want to accidentally step on you."

Janet smiled and tried her best to get in a comfortable position lying on the floor, finally choosing to try to nap on her side. "Go ahead, I'm ready," she said to David.

"Okay, lights out," David said, as he flicked the switch and the room fell into total darkness. "Okay, I'm trying not to step on you. You know, maybe I'll just crawl, it seems a little safer."

Janet heard David moving in the dark and finally settling on a spot up next to her. "Good night," he said.

"Good night," Janet replied. Within minutes, both of them were sleeping.

CHAPTER 10

Janet and David both awoke abruptly to the sound of the trapdoor opening.

"Oh, my," they heard Kelly say, "What naughty things are you kids up to with the lights turned off. You might want to turn them on. I bring gifts."

David crawled on his hands and knees to where the light switch was and flicked it on. The harsh light of the fluorescents seemed brighter than ever as they both tried to look up to where Kelly was standing.

"Oh, I'm sorry. You two were taking a nap together. Hope there wasn't any hanky-panky going on." Kelly really seemed to be enjoying her job as prison warden. Or whatever it was that she had become.

"I want you both to step back away from the trapdoor. I'm going to lower a couple of things down in a bucket. And provided my 'rope' doesn't break, you two will be able to have yourselves a little party."

Party? Janet thought. What the hell? But both Janet and David complied and stepped back. Neither of them wanted to make Kelly any more pissed off than she already was.

"Okay, everybody clear? Incoming!"

David and Janet watched as a plastic bucket was slowly lowered to the floor by—what *was* that tied to the bucket? It looked like some weird multi-color scarf knitted badly together, which, as it turned out, it was.

"Do you like my pretty scarf I made? Yeah, it has been a little boring, just sitting around doing nothing all day, so I made a scarf. I hope that the scarf stays together long enough to get this bucket down to the ground. Almost there, great!" Kelly said, and dropped the other end of the scarf into the hole. Oh, and I have one more present for you."

A few seconds later, what looked like a blanket fell down from the trapdoor and landed on the ground. "I hear it is going to be a little cold tonight and I don't want my two bestest guests getting cold." Before either Janet or David could open their mouths to speak, the door slammed closed and they were alone together again.

"Wow, is it just me, or are you also just a little scared to look in the bucket? I wonder what her idea of a party is?" Janet said as she walked across the room to where the red bucket sat. "Nice scarf," she snorted as she untied it from the handle of the bucket. Looking at the mangled scarf, Janet thought to herself that a crappy scarf would keep her warmer than no scarf, so she quickly grabbed for the scarf on the floor and wrapped it around her neck. Mine now. Inside the bucket, strangely enough, were a big bottle of Jack Daniels and two large bags of potato chips. "Okay, how did she know I hate whiskey?" Janet said, as she passed the bottle over to David. "Potato chips, those I like. And look, a dirty twin-sized blanket. Oh, and don't forget the awesome bucket. Oh joy, oh joy! We can use it as our toilet. We are going to party tonight. Or today. I couldn't tell what time it was when she opened the door."

"I'm going to guess it is about 5 pm or something? I seriously could use an alcoholic drink about now. How about you? How about some Jack?" David asked as he twisted the bottle open. "As there are no cups, I hope you don't mind if I drink from the bottle?"

"Be my guest," Janet said, gesturing as if the bottle were full of poison. "I have to tell you, the only liquor she could have possibly lowered down to us that would have been worse would be tequila. Or possibly brandy." Janet shivered and made a gagging noise.

"Okay, but you're missing out." David grabbed the bottle with both hands and tilted it up. He took a giant drink from the bottle, and as Janet watched the bubbles forming and breaking in the bottle, the liquid disappeared down David's throat. After drinking more of the crap in one drink than Janet had in her whole life, David lowered the bottle, shivered a little, and made a face. "Ahhhh... good stuff. This is just what I needed. Sure you don't want a drink?"

David moved the bottle over to Janet's reach. Janet could smell the whiskey and she almost gagged.

"Um, no thanks. I'll just eat the chips." Janet sat down on the floor and ripped open one of the potato chip bags, pulled a chip out and shoved it into her mouth. "Oh my god, food of the gods. Oh, they are so salty and good. Oh, this is my bag. You can have the other one." Janet made a big production out of pulling her bag of chips out of David's reach.

"Oh sure, hog the chips. Go ahead. Mr. Daniels and I are going to get acquainted. If there is any time in my life that I've wanted and needed a drink more, today is the day." David proceeded to drink another inch of liquid out of the big bottle, to Janet's guesstimation.

"Good thing she gave us a bucket. Because if you keep drinking like that, you are going to be a little vomity pretty soon." Janet smiled, but in her head, she was kind of worried for David. He must be so stressed out about everything, but alcohol wasn't the answer. Yeah, thanks Kelly, some "gift," Janet thought. Kelly is truly an evil person, Janet was beginning to think, but I got to love her for sending down the chips for us. Looking at David, Janet could tell that the whiskey was already starting to hit him, and why not? Neither of them had had hardly anything to eat or drink. Janet thought she might be able to get drunk on one sip.

"Oh, what the hell. I'll have a drink," Janet said to David, and indicated to him that she wanted the bottle. "You only live once, right?"

David smiled. "Absolutely," he said, and handed the bottle in Janet's direction. She took the bottle out of David's hand and then wiped the mouth of it off with her shirt.

"Germs, you know," she said teasingly. She plugged her nose while trying with one and a half hands to steady the bottle up to her mouth for a drink.

As soon as the brown liquid hit her throat, Janet knew that taking a drink of this stuff had been a bad idea. Still, she took three more swallows before she pulled the bottle quickly away from her lips. "Bleah!" Janet said, and with that, she started coughing, almost throwing up as she struggled to keep the vile liquid down.

"Could they make anything more disgusting? I don't think so. Feels like it's eating a hole in my stomach." After a few more shivers and faces, Janet grabbed her bag of chips and started stuffing them in her mouth, trying to make the horrible taste of the whiskey go away.

"Wow, way to go Janet!" David said loudly. "I like a party girl." David tried to give her a high five, but Janet didn't know it was coming and David totally missed his mark. "We'll have to work on that," David said, smiling more broadly than Janet had ever remembered him doing. He was definitely well on his way to the Land of Inebriates.

David finally put down the bottle of whiskey and grabbed the bag of chips. Putting his hands on either side of the bag, he yanked the bag open and of course he pulled too hard and chips flew everywhere. "Thirty-second rule," David said quickly, as he stooped down, grabbed a large handful from the floor, and stuffed it into his mouth.

David ate the chips with his mouth open. After a few chews, he opened his mouth more and said, "Ummm, nature's pepper!" With that comment, David sprayed potato chips coated in whiskey all over Janet's face.

"Whoops!" said David, as he comically tried to cover his mouth after the fact. "Here," he said, grabbing the scarf. "Let me clean that off for you." The scarf was already up to her face before Janet could react, adding yarn fuzz to the already icky mess that was there.

Janet quickly stood up and moved a few steps away to grab the toilet paper; with a few sheets, she furiously scrubbed, trying to wipe the spit and the chips and the whiskey and the yarn fuzz off of her face. Yuck. She even felt like some of it got in her mouth. Holy shit, she thought, he was getting drunk. Janet was more than a little worried.

"Okay then," said Janet. "Why don't we slow down a little." Janet grabbed the whiskey bottle and held it tightly against her body, away from David's reach.

"Whatever," David said, and proceeded to stuff even more potato chips into his already full mouth.

Janet slowly slid the bottle behind her back, trying to hide the whiskey from David so maybe he wouldn't see it for a while and he would slow down a bit. "Hey David, you never told me about your job. What is it exactly you do?"

David lifted his eyes up from the bag of chips and Janet could see by his eyes that he really didn't need any more liquor.

"Well, Janet, if I can call you that. At my job, I take pieces of paper from the inbox, type what they say into mister computer, and then I put the pieces of paper into the inbox... I mean outbox. That... is what my job entails."

"That must be interesting. Do you like your job?" Janet was really trying to keep the topic going as long as she could.

"Like my job? I absolutely LOVE my job. Best job in the world. Who wouldn't love my job? I will tell you who, me, that's who. My stupid motherfucking boss Don is such an asshole and his job—a fucking squirrel could do his job better than he does… no offense to squirrels." David wiped his mouth off with the back of his hand and burped.

Janet tried to kind of stand back and just watch the train wreck. David clearly wasn't used to drinking and really couldn't hold his liquor. He was going to have a monster headache tomorrow.

All of the sudden he yelled, "Where is that fucking bitch Kelly? KELLY!" he yelled, loud enough to wake the dead. "KELLY! KELLY! Where the hell are you? I HAVE YOUR STUPID STUD MUFFIN KEVIN WITH ME. HE WANTS TO FUCK!"

With this last statement, David put his finger up to his lips and made a shushing noise. "Shhhh, I'm trying to trick her. Kevin isn't here. He is gone. Poor Kevin. Couldn't stand the competition."

David started to look around. "Where's my whiskey? Where did I put my whiskey?" He looked bleary eyed toward Janet and pointed his finger at her. "I know who has my whiskey. Janet does. Janet, are you playing a game with me? I can find it you know… you can't hide it from me, Janet."

David tried to get to his feet, but stumbled back down to his knees before finally standing. "Janet. I need the whiskey. Please?"

Oh, what the heck, thought Janet. Maybe he will drink himself into a stupor. I'm sick of babysitting him. Janet took the bottle and handed it over to David. "All yours, David."

"Of course it's mine. It always has been all mine. Kelly, the stupid bitch tried to give away what was mine. And tried to hide it from me." David put the bottle up to his lips and took a bunch of swallows. "You know, Janet, all women are whores. Oops, wait a minute…. *You* are a woman. Ha, ha! Didn't mean you, Janet. I'm sure you are not a whore."

"No offense taken, David. I'm not a whore. Say anything you want. You are so drunk, you won't remember it in the morning." Janet was starting to seriously dislike David. Maybe she had misjudged him? No, she really wanted to give him the benefit of the doubt. He was hurting. And drinking whiskey seemed to make it all feel better for him somehow.

"Hey, David, can I have another drink?" Janet put out her hand and tried to grab for the bottle.

"You want another drink? Sure, you can have another drink. Let's sit down here on the floor and get drunk together and talk about all the whores in the world."

Against her better judgment, Janet sat on the floor close to where David was slumped and took the bottle from his hands. After wiping off the opening again with her shirt, she put the bottle up to her lips and pretended to take a big drink. David wasn't fooled.

"You didn't drink. I saw it. You didn't drink. You have to take a drink. That is the rule." Before he could grab the bottle again, Janet put it back up to her lips and this time really took a drink. David smiled in satisfaction. "There you go, Janet. See, not so bad after all."

Janet took the bottle away from her lips and started choking. "I think I'm going to be sick," she said. She stood up and staggered over to the bucket with the bottle still in her hands. She made a few retching sounds, and thinking David was too drunk to notice, started to pour the whiskey into the bucket.

"Hey, hey! You're spilling it. Stupid whore—give me that bottle!" David staggered across the room. As he reached to take the bottle from Janet's hands, he clumsily hit it instead. The bottle flew across the room and crashed against the wall.

David and Janet watched as the glass and the liquid slowly slid down the wall. "You fucking bitch. You shouldn't have done that." With that, David backhanded Janet so hard across the face that she flew and hit the ground, her head hitting the cement with a horrible thumping sound.

Janet lay there where she fell, stunned. I can't freaking believe he hit me. *Oh, my god, he is so going to regret that.* Janet tried to focus and get up, but found she could see stars in her field of vision. Her head hurt so bad that every time she tried to sit up she got dizzy and had to put her head back down.

"I'm sorry, David," Janet said from the floor. She tried to lie convincingly. "I'm sorry the bottle got broken. I was going to give it to you… I really was…." Janet stopped at this point and put her hands solidly against the floor. The room seemed to be spinning. I think I'm really hurt, Janet thought to herself, and she closed her eyes to make the spinning stop.

"Oh, get up, you stupid bitch… I didn't hit you that hard. Women are always like this. Oh my, he hit me. Then crying with snot pouring down their faces. I am so sick of women. You are probably just pretending, like my stupid wife tried to… always pretending she was asleep so I wouldn't touch her. Didn't help her out much."

Janet opened her eyes and tried to get her bearings. This situation was way out of hand, she had had no idea David was anything like the monster standing over her. She had never been hit by a man and was having a hard time getting over the shock that yes, that motherfucker really did hit me.

"David, it's okay. I know you didn't try to hurt me. It was just a reflex because I broke your bottle. I am so sorry—I didn't mean to let it break. It is entirely all my fault. I am so sorry." Janet hoped her apology and blaming herself for the bottle breaking would appease David enough that he would settle down.

"Damn right, it's all your fault. And I just hit you out of reflex. I couldn't help it. Any man would have done the same thing." David brushed his hair back from his forehead and then turned to look at the broken mess that once was his bottle of whiskey. "Crap, a fucking almost full bottle of whiskey, wasted. Man that pisses me off. We were just getting the party started."

David made a little dance, twisting his body around and saying, "Party, come on, let's party." After a few seconds of this, he said, "I got to take a piss." Rather than go over to the bucket, he walked over to the corner where the bucket wasn't and proceeded to pee all over the floor.

Janet had pulled herself up so that while she was still too dizzy to stand, she had managed to get her elbows up underneath her so she could see. Watching David peeing all over the floor and himself… Janet stopped and wondered how the heck she had gotten herself into this mess. Then her mind turned to Kelly and she finally figured it out.

Kelly, she thought. Kelly knew that with the whiskey he would get filthy drunk and turn from this nice guy he pretended to be into this slimy drunken thing in front of her. Huh, Janet though. I wonder if this is what Kelly's life had been like? Was he always like this? How did she cope? I would have so been out the door the first time he hit me. Which Janet wished she could do now, but couldn't since she was in a hole in the ground and all. She had to somehow, very carefully, think of a way to try to calm David down until he passed out, which judging by the way he was struggling to zip up his pants should be pretty soon.

"Ahhhh, feel like a new man," David said as he hitched up his pants a little and walked over to where Janet was still lying. "So, Janet," David said as he roughly sat on the floor next to her, "what do you like to do for fun?" His face was so close to hers, with unbrushed teeth and the smell of the whiskey on his breath, that Janet almost vomited. She didn't know what a concussion felt like, but she was pretty sure she had one.

"I bet," David said creepily, "I bet you like to get kinky. Did I guess your secret? Oh, Janet. She acts so prim and proper on the surface and she is probably really a wildcat in bed. So, am I right, Janet? Are you a wildcat in bed?"

David lurched much closer to Janet, with his far hand reached out. He grabbed at her left breast and squeezed it… hard. Janet screamed out in agony and tried to fight him off. The pain had brought her situation clearly into focus. She was in trouble. Janet tried to think through the pain; she had to control this insanity of David's somehow before something even worse happened.

"David, I'm married with two kids. You don't want me. I'm old. You deserve someone nice and beautiful, like that blonde you were telling me about with the panties. Please David, don't. You're hurting me." Janet looked up into David's face, but he didn't look like the same David anymore. It was as if his brain had gone somewhere else.

"Shhhh…. Shhhh…. Oooh, she likes to pretend she doesn't want it. I know you want it." With that, he squeezed her nipple hard and climbed so that he was up over the top of her. Janet stifled her scream as best she could, but the pain was unbearable.

"David, please, David. Don't do this. Please?" Janet wished with every fiber of her being that her head didn't hurt so much. That she could kick him or scratch him or rip out his hair to somehow make him stop what he was doing. But she felt like she was having a hard enough time staying conscious. Janet was very beyond just being scared. Janet was desperate.

"David, let's have sex. I want to have sex with you. I've thought about it since the first time we saw each other. That's probably why Kelly was so mad. She could see the chemistry between us." Janet didn't want to be raped, but she started to think there was no way she was getting out of this without a miracle.

"Oh, you had to go and bring up my stupid whore wife Kelly. God, she is so frigid. After we got married, she never wanted to have sex. But then I figured out, she just liked to pretend she didn't want to have sex. So I gave her what she wanted, a fight. I bet that's what you want too, isn't it, Janet? A little fight, a little rough sex… okay, if that is what you want."

David grabbed on to Janet's sweater and her bra with both hands and pulled the front of her clothing down hard, until it was underneath her breasts. "Oh, nice titties," he said. "Yummy." As Janet screamed "No!" and then started to cry, he lowered his head down and started slobbering all over her breasts.

Janet was repulsed. He was disgusting and gross and she couldn't get him off of her, he was holding her down so hard with the weight of his body, he felt twice as heavy as he looked. Oh my god, he is going to rape me. Janet thought of the only parts of her body that she felt she had control of. Looking down, she moaned and tried to act as if she was enjoying what he was doing. This made David stop what he was doing and look up at her face. Janet was all smiles, so he allowed her to pull his head up, away from her breasts and up to her face for a kiss. David kissed at her mouth, almost licking it more than kissing it. And then, not to be distracted, he again moved down to her neck.

Before he had a chance to react, Janet shifted her head down so that her face was below his head, and with her mouth she bit him as hard as she could on his shoulder, grabbing as much of the meat of it as she could between her teeth. David swatted at Janet's face and mouth in vain, but that didn't work to make her release her bite. He pushed her head violently away from him, but that only managed to make his agony worse. In desperation, David took his fingers and somehow jammed them into Janet's mouth, then wiggled and wiggled them until he was finally able to get her teeth pried open just enough to pull his shoulder flesh from her mouth. Screaming in rage and in pain, David totally lost it. He took Janet's head in his hands and violently started throwing it back, again and again, against the hard concrete floor. Janet blacked out after the third hit.

CHAPTER 11

Scratching...she heard scratching ... or something. Janet had been having the best dream about standing on a hill, looking out over the scrub brush of the prairie, not a person or house in sight, the warm winds blowing her hair around her face. Just standing out there, so peaceful. And then there was the scratching that wasn't part of the dream. Janet tried to open her eyes, but for some reason she couldn't. It was as if they weren't listening to her. Janet tried to listen again for the strange noise, but she couldn't hear anything. It was quiet now. She felt like she was floating in a vast nothingness, and that seemed like a good thing. Janet tried to have more thoughts, but her mind shut down and she drifted off to sleep again.

For a time, Janet drifted in and out of consciousness, each time trying to make sense of images flashing through her brain. Starbucks, that's right. I was at Starbucks. Why was I at Starbucks? I don't go out of my way to drink their expensive drinks. And really, did any of them have actual coffee in them anymore? So, she was at Starbucks and she kind of remembered a face, a man's face; he looked kind of familiar, but she couldn't place him. I think his name was David? Yes, that was his name. Okay, so why was she at Starbucks with some guy named David? Janet tried to think, but the pain in her head was unbearable.

What had she done to her head? None of this made sense; Janet tried very hard to think as she struggled to open her eyes. After a few seconds, she got her right eye to partially open, but she quickly shut it because the intense light made her head feel even worse. After a minute or so had passed, she decided to try opening her right eye or maybe even both eyes again, and finally she managed to get them both opened a little. About one foot away in front of her face was a cement wall. What? Where the hell was she?

Janet tried to remember, but the memories were in just bits and pieces, jumbled in her brain, flowing from one image to another, none of it making sense. There was a car ride, and a trap door, and a gun... okay, now that didn't make any sense. Maybe she was remembering a movie she had just seen? After her eyes couldn't take the task of seeing anymore, she closed them, and decided to try and flip over and look the other way. She slowly started to turn her head, but just as she had almost gotten her head to the point where she thought she should now be seeing up, she noticed that the back of her head felt like mush. And then it started to hurt. Holy crap her head hurt. It felt like an overripe jack-o-lantern that had stayed too long on the step after Halloween. Soft and squishy and wet. And with that squishy feeling, there was an indescribable pain.

Janet didn't want to stop the rotation of her head there, where the pain of her head was so great. Since she had already seen what was on the other side of her, she grimly kept moving her head over to look the opposite way. Again, she felt cold cement on her cheek, but this time it was on the other side of her face from the one on which she had woken up. After a deep breath or two, Janet tried to sneak her eyelids up just a tiny bit. In front of her head was something that looked like dark hair. Oily, dark hair...was it Eddie? Janet didn't think so; the color didn't seem right. Her mind flashed back to the Starbucks and the person sitting across the table from her. It was that guy David, it was David's head...she was sure of that.

Memories started rushing back to her: how she had met David in the coffee shop to talk about his house and a robbery of some sort. How they had left and his wife... Kelly... had kidnapped them? What the hell... was she confusing real life with the movie of the week? And she remembered driving for what seemed like days, and then stopping, and then darkness. And then she remembered dragging something heavy... a body? No, that couldn't be. And then she also remembered climbing down a ladder into a dark space that was a hole in the ground and then the door to the hole being closed above her, making it become darker than she had ever thought possible.

As she was thinking, she heard the head beside her (David?) making a noise that almost sounded like someone who has a really bad cold. It was kind of a snorting, sniffling noise and then it was quiet again. Janet was just too exhausted. She had done all the thinking her brain could do for the moment and so she decided to close her eyes again just for a second. And then, just as quickly, she fell back into a deep sleep.

As she drifted back into consciousness for a brief moment, something in her head unlocked the door she had hidden her recent memories behind; and beyond that door, she suddenly remembered. He raped me! Oh my god, the motherfucker David raped me. He knocked me unconscious and then.... Oh my god. He was sick! The memory of the night before (or was it still the same night?) had come rushing back to her brain when it was just at the edge of being asleep and being awake.

She remembered how David had gotten really drunk, and how he then had turned nasty and ugly and how he had hit her, and she vaguely remembered hitting the ground hard. All these thoughts in her head—it was too much. Janet felt so sick with the thoughts of what had happened to her that the little bit that was still in her stomach came out of her mouth and puddled on the ground next to her face. She couldn't move, so her head rested in the puddle of vomit.

Janet didn't remember the rape, other than that it had happened, but her body was slowly telling her that something was definitely wrong. Her breasts, she noticed first, felt bruised and battered, as if they had been beaten or something. And then as she slowly moved her thoughts lower down her body, and tried to shift her hips to ease the pain she felt, she could feel a much bigger pain growing down in the space between her legs, a pain that intensified with every second, so much so that she wished she could pass out again to escape it. Oh, please, God, why? I'm a good person. I didn't ask for this. Fucking David. He wasn't a person. He was a monster. Wearing human skin.

She wished she had Kelly's gun, because at that moment she felt she could have shot him, shot him again and again until he would never be able to do something like this ever again. Dead, dead, dead. Her whole body hurt so much… but still she felt numb in places from the coldness of the floor. It was then that Janet realized she didn't have her jeans on, or her underwear. She was naked from the waist down, her whole lower body exposed, bruised and bleeding and lying on a cold cement floor. Janet shivered uncontrollably with the cold. Where the blanket was, she had no idea. But she knew she had to find a way to get warm quickly.

Down by her bare feet, Janet thought she could feel with her toes what must be her jeans. After gingerly testing the leg to find out how well she could cope with the pain, she attempted to slowly move her foot closer to the jeans. Then, with her toes, she was able to grab a piece of the cloth and slowly very slowly raise the jeans up to where her hands could reach them. She pulled the jeans upwards with her hands so that she could now see them. Thankfully, Janet saw that her underwear was scrunched up just inside the waistband. Now she only needed to somehow find a way get her clothing on, without making the pain in her body exponentially worse.

Sitting up was out of the question. The pain of trying to get her head vertical … she knew that was going to make the agony in her head and her body much worse. After a bit of thought, she pulled the underwear out of the jeans, put a hand on either side, and slowly lowered them down to her waist, while at the same time she pulled up her knees and feet to meet her hands halfway. It hurt so much, so very much, but Janet was determined to get her underwear back on somehow. Finally, after a painful struggle, her toes felt the edge of the elastic of the waistband of the underwear; she put one foot in and through the leg hole opening, and then she did the same with the other foot. Again, slowly she eased her legs back down and as she did, the underwear slid up her legs. Arching her back as much as she could stand to, she finally pulled the underwear up the rest of the way. It felt so good to have something covering her, but she was still cold and still feeling very exposed and vulnerable, lying there with just her underwear on.

Now she needed to get her jeans on somehow, too. After a little deliberation, she realized there was no way she was going to avoid the pain. With a deep breath, she slowly repeated the process she had done with her underwear to put on her jeans. After she had somehow gotten both legs into the opening of the pants, she began to pull them up. As the crotch seam of the jeans slowly encountered the space between her legs, she winced and finally realized the extent of how much she had been injured. Not wanting to—but needing to—she pulled the jeans up the rest of the way, zipped and buttoned them, and then slowly laid her head back down, rolling it to the side facing the wall.

Tears of pain, anger, humiliation, and grief started to sneak out of her eyes, and though she tried not to let herself cry, there was no stopping it. So she cried quietly, and after a while, she finally cried herself back to sleep.

CHAPTER 12

"Time to wake up, sleepy head," Janet heard from a voice that that seemed like it was very close to her ear. "Wake up Janet, come on sweetie. You already missed breakfast. And it's almost lunch."

David. Janet opened her eyes to find him with his face about 12 inches from her own face. His breath smelled horrible, like whiskey and potato chips and vomit. Janet froze. She was so afraid of him after what he had so violently done to her that she couldn't even begin to think what she should do or say.

"Ahhh, there you are. Thought you were going to sleep all day." David smiled and reached forward and flipped a piece of Janet's hair back away from her face. Janet flinched. "Some party we had last night, huh?" David said and laughed. "So you like the rough sex, don't you? I could tell by the way you were fighting a little bit, like you really didn't want it. But I knew. Kelly used to be like that in the beginning, put on this great performance of struggling and fighting before we finally made love. But then the stupid bitch stopped. She just lay there like a cold fish, no matter what I did. Frigid bitch."

Janet blinked her eyes a little bit. She could not believe what she was hearing. David called that violent attack that he had done to her *sex*? He hit me and knocked me unconscious and then he violently raped me while I lay there helpless—how could that be *sex*? This person, this new David, was a person she had never wanted to know and wished she had never even met, let alone be stuck with him in an underground dungeon.

"Here," David said as he got up a bit and reached off to the side. "I bet you would like some water. I don't know about you, but I have the worst cottonmouth ever." David unscrewed the lid of the water bottle and held it out to her.

Janet didn't move. She couldn't believe this was the same monster from last night. Was he two different people? How could two such separate people live in one body? He was definitely a psychopath, or a maniac, or... just a fucking sadistic twisted creep. He sure had had her fooled.

"No water just right yet? Okay, I'll just put it here beside you and you can decide when you're ready to take a drink. Trust me, you'll feel much better after you drink some of that." David put the lid back on the bottle and set it down near the top of Janet's head.

"I wish we had a mirror. You should see yourself. I tried to clean your face off a little bit for you this morning... you had gunk everywhere. You look a little better, but you've got a nasty bruise on your cheek from when I had to hit you. But, in a couple of days, you will forget it was even ever there." David pulled himself up so his back was against the wall and he leaned there, as if he was sitting on a deck chair on the beach enjoying the sunset or something.

Janet closed her eyes and tried to think back. Had there been any signs that he was a lunatic rapist? She couldn't think of anything. Except that one off-hand remark he had made about women being stupid. Huh. And then there was his wife Kelly, who was extremely pissed at him for some reason, so pissed that she pulled a gun on him, tasered him, kidnapped him, and threw him down into this hole, like he was a piece of garbage or something. But why did she grab Janet too? Had that been part of her plan all along, grab his "girlfriend" along with him so she could have some extra help, or fun or "leverage," or was I just in the wrong place at the wrong time? And the big, *big* question was... what exactly did Kelly plan to do with them? She couldn't keep us in this hole indefinitely, could she? Just continue to throw down food and water and keep us captive and for how long? She had to have a plan. Everything else she did so far seemed so planned out, she must have some plan in the works for them.

Something else was bothering Janet. The Jack Daniels "party." That was such an unexpected and out-of-character thing for Kelly to do, it was almost like a gift for David or something. Had Kelly known that the real David would show himself to Janet when he drank too much? As his wife, she had to have known something like this would happen. And if she did, she was a monster too.

Janet really wished she could talk to Kelly. Actually, she really just wished to tie her up tightly first and then question her. Janet needed to find out if this is what Kelly's home life had been like. Is this why she had eventually cheated on David? Or did the beatings start after Kelly cheated on him? Janet's head hurt with all the possibilities and questions swirling around in her brain.

But, first things first. She needed to somehow heal and get her strength back quickly. As a self-preservation measure, she decided it might be a better tactic to pretend to go along with David's "rough sex" story. Confronting him down here was a stupid and reckless lose-lose situation. She was trapped here with him and he could do the same thing to her again—or worse. Janet knew that somehow she needed to feel that she was in control again. With that thought, Janet took a deep breath and tried to sit up.

"Do you need some help there? Looks like you're still a little woozy from the drinking we did last night. Here, let me help you." David reached around Janet's waist and very carefully pulled her up into a sitting position. "There you go. You okay?" David asked her gently. Janet nodded her head in a slow yes. "So, ready to try some water now?" Janet again nodded her head yes; she didn't trust herself to speak yet.

David opened the bottle and held it up so Janet could reach it. Slowly, very slowly, Janet moved her arm up, grasped the bottle with her hand, and put it up to her lips.

Janet drank the water from the bottle in small sips. With those first small sips, it didn't seem like any water made it to her throat for her to actually swallow, her mouth was so incredibly dry. After about the fourth sip, Janet could feel the water sliding down her sore throat and then making it to her stomach. Janet really, really hoped she didn't throw up with this water; she needed it. And the thought of throwing up with this much pain in her head made her pull the bottle away from her lips and wait for a few minutes to make sure the water she had already drunk was going to stay down.

"Thanks," Janet said to David with a small voice. She even tried to add a smile, but it hurt her face to make even that tiny movement. David, the asshole rapist, smiled back.

"I'm glad you're awake and drinking some water. I was worried about you there for a while. But now you seem fine, just a little slow, still. Once 'Doctor David' takes care of you, you'll be as good as new."

Janet shuddered at the thought that at this point, with her injuries, she was totally dependent on David. She scanned her eyes around the room, trying to find something to look at to avoid having to look at David. She could see where the bottle of booze had hit the wall and shattered into a million pieces. Glass was everywhere. Seeing that and with no other choice, she asked David for help. "Could you please get me my socks and my boots? My feet are cold."

David jumped up without a moment's hesitation. "At your service ma'am," he said, and then he scooped up her boots and grabbed her socks off the shelf where she had left them to dry. "And, we wouldn't want your cute little feet stepping on some glass, would we." He looked at her with a blank look on his face and handed her the boots and socks.

Janet struggled to get the socks on. Sliding her toes into the cotton fabric and slowly pulling them up her legs, she realized how cold she really was and with the warmth of the fabric, her feet once again started to feel better. The boots were not as easy to get on as the socks. Luckily, they zipped up the side and with a little struggle because her feet were so swollen from the cold, she got both of them on. With a sigh of relief, Janet was happy that she was finally fully dressed. She felt a tiny bit safer with all of her clothes on, a little more secure. But just a tiny bit.

"So, along with water, my lovely wife Kelly provided us with two oranges and for each of us a bagel. No cream cheese or anything. Couldn't do that now... could we bitch Kelly!" David loudly directed the last part of his statement up toward the trapdoor. "Do you want me to peel your orange for you?" David asked Janet before he passed her food on to her.

The thought of David taking his dirty disgusting hands and then sticking his fingernails in her orange was out of the question. So after a while, when her hands started to remember how to work, Janet got the orange peeled, pulled off a piece, and shoved it into her mouth.

Oh my god, this is the best orange ever, Janet thought as she savored the sweet juice in her mouth before swallowing. After eating two small sections, Janet felt a little queasy, but that soon passed and after a few minutes, she discovered she had eaten the whole fruit. She took a quick sip of the water and then eyed the bagel, which was tucked neatly into a Ziploc sandwich bag. After a brief discussion with her brain, she decided it was probably a good idea to put something into her stomach other than just the acidic orange. She opened the bag, slowly ripped small pieces off of the bagel, and put them in her mouth. She made sure she chewed each piece in her mouth well enough so the bagel wouldn't get stuck halfway when it went down her sore throat. After half a bagel, she decided to take a rest.

"So, what time is it?" Janet asked, trying her best not to let on through her eyes, or with the tone of her voice, how much she was now extremely repulsed by the man in front of her.

David looked at her with a cocked head and searched her face, as if he was looking for something. After apparently finding nothing, he commented, "You really must have been out of it. I told you earlier that you had missed breakfast and that it was almost lunchtime already. You don't remember that?" David seemed almost a little peeved at having to repeat the information again.

It was all she could do for Janet not to snap back at David's peevishness, with a *gee, maybe she wouldn't be so confused if some super psycho named David hadn't beat her head against the ground until she was unconscious and then raped her.* But she held back; she could and would wait to have her say with him later. Janet seriously hoped "the lunch drop" was soon. She wanted to get near the trap door so Kelly could at least see her, see her battered face, so that she would know what her husband had done to her. Something within Kelly still had to have some compassion, right? With this thought in mind, Janet started the process of somehow starting to stand up.

Janet's head was pounding; it felt mushy… like a bad cantaloupe. Nevertheless, she knew she had to save herself some way, since she now knew that David was in no way the person to rely on to get her out of this hole. Janet started to slide her feet up toward her body, and then she pushed up with her legs as hard as she could until she was almost in a crouched sitting position. So far, so good. She wished she had something to pull herself up with, but the only thing that was available was the wall behind her back.

After repositioning her body so she was now pushing the bulk of her weight up against the wall, she slowly, very slowly, stood up. This isn't so hard, Janet thought to herself, piece of cake. But as she finally stood erect with her knees straightened, she started to feel dizzy. The back of her head accidentally brushed against the cement wall. Sharp flashes of pain stabbed into her brain and seemed to travel all the way down her body and then back up. Reflexively, Janet grabbed for stability and unfortunately, the only thing to grab was David.

"Whoa, there," David said, as he tried to keep Janet upright. "See, I told you with Dr. David taking care of you, you would be better in no time. However, I think that was enough exercise for a while. Here, let me help you get back down into a sitting position. I'm going to grab you around the waist and help you." Janet allowed David to hold her waist as he slowly and surprisingly gently guided her to the floor.

"Thanks," Janet said quietly without looking at David. She was exhausted. Janet slid her body down, until she was once again lying on her side. She needed to sleep—that was all she wanted. All she could think of in her foggy brain was going back to sleep. And it seemed as if her dreams were answered, because her head no sooner touched the cement than she swiftly drifted off, into a deep and much-needed sleep.

As Janet slept, she dreamt fitfully. In her dream, people were chasing her and touching her and she kept brushing their hands off of her body but the people wouldn't stop touching her. And then, suddenly the dream changed, the people weren't chasing her anymore but now she noticed that she could feel cold, wet dirt all around her, the weight of it almost pinning her in. She could still see the sky above her, so she knew she was finally out of the dungeon when suddenly, the dirt around gave way and started crumbling in on her. First it was just a light dusting, but pretty soon the speed of the collapse increased until more and more dirt was raining down on her, falling on her face and in her eyes, and as she opened up her mouth to scream for help, her mouth started filling with dirt. She was slowly suffocating, slowly being buried alive. Janet started frantically clawing at the dirt with her now-trapped hands, trying to get up, but with each movement, it was getting harder and harder. She knew she was about to die.

"Hey, hey! It's okay. You're just having a bad dream, nothing to worry about. You are still safe and sound with me. I will take good care of you." David stroked Janet's face. He had seen her moving in her sleep and tried to comfort her, and soon she had calmed enough to stop thrashing. After the nightmare disappeared from her brain, there were no more dreams for Janet... just blissful sleep.

A little while later, Janet woke up, feeling more rested than she had in a long while. It is amazing how deep sleep can make you feel so much better, so much more whole, Janet thought. Finally, Janet opened her eyes, turned her head, and saw David beside her. Once again, the nausea returned. So much for feeling better.

Janet still felt sick to her stomach, but she felt almost like her head was just a bit more solid and that the pain had gotten somehow more bearable. She took a closer look at David and realized that he was sleeping. Thank God that in one way, at least, he was a typical guy and could sleep anytime, anywhere. Janet really wanted to get up and practice walking, without having to listen to that prick chiming along at her with false praise: "You're doing great, Janet!" Yes, and I would be doing a whole hell of a lot "greater," Janet thought, if you hadn't beat the shit out of me and raped me, you sadistic shithead.

Janet saw that there were new food and drink items sitting on the floor next to her half-eaten bagel, still inside the sandwich bag. Shit, Janet thought, she had slept through lunch. She had wanted to be there at the opening of the trapdoor so the bitch Kelly could see firsthand what her asshole husband had done to her. Oh well, she still might have one more chance before the day was through. But this time, if any booze was coming down in a pail, she was breaking the bottle to smithereens *before* David could put his little grubby hands on it.

Janet gingerly pulled herself into a sitting position. Sleeping on the hard concrete floor in any situation would be almost unbearable. Sleeping on one when you were kidnapped, raped, starved, cold, and seriously injured was a whole different nightmare unto itself. Fortunately, the human body does its best to endure, usually without any of our futile human help. Eventually, sleep takes hold. It's the glue that keeps us functioning and sane and whole. Without it, we wouldn't exist.

Janet slowly stood up. Okay, she was now vertical, step one completed. But standing up on her feet soon made Janet feel woozy, nauseous, and supremely unsteady. Slowly, slowly she made herself move and began to shuffle over to the side of the room. She wanted to be able to use the wall for support while she walked; falling down right now would not be a good thing. Upon reaching the wall, which wasn't that far away, Janet allowed herself to rest a few seconds. Nevertheless, she was determined to make it to the far wall of the room and back. She needed to be able to walk, so she might be somewhat more able to protect herself... and to be more able to escape, she hoped, if that time ever came.

The first couple of steps weren't too bad. The dizziness was the worst thing. Janet continued and got closer to the far wall. While it was still only about eight feet away, to Janet it seemed more like 800 feet. At about that point in her walk, Janet could feel herself start to feel nauseous again. Okay, Janet thought, with my limited medical knowledge, I'm thinking I definitely have a concussion. That isn't good. Wasn't she supposed to keep herself awake for 24 hours or something? Why she was supposed to do that, she didn't know. Maybe it was so her brain wouldn't die while she slept. What a comforting thought. However, she had made it this far and Janet had one trait that would serve her well in this situation: pissed-offed-ness. Janet could not stand being taking advantage of, in any situation. In school, it had made her excel to get better grades, to be the most admired and respected person that she could in her class. And in her adult life, God protect anybody that stepped on her toes to better their own advantage. She would run them to the ground.

Finally, Janet made it to the other side of the room. One small victory, yeah. Okay, and now back. Janet kept this up, walking painfully back and forth, from one side of the cell to the other, until she was pretty sure she had done ten laps. Thankfully, the movement was actually starting to help, because at about the fourth lap, she didn't need to hold the wall anymore. But again later, on the final lap, she wouldn't have made it if the wall hadn't been there for her to lean against. She was gasping for breath and sweating by the time she finished. Oh, come on Janet, she thought. There is no way you are that out of shape. There was nothing like giving yourself a little pep talk, to make sure that you could keep yourself alive if need be.

Janet sat back down on the floor, making sure she had positioned herself a little further away from David. Looking over at him, Janet couldn't believe that two such very different beings could exist in one body. I know alcohol sometimes makes people do crazy things they wouldn't normally do. But savagely beating and raping someone... that was beyond crazy. Note to self, Janet thought. Before I decide on making new friends with anybody, I want to watch what they are like when they are plastered while safe and in a large crowd, before somehow finding myself alone with them. Janet shook her head in disgust and angrily flipped her middle finger at David. Small satisfaction. David kept sleeping.

Okay, now that I know I can walk, I need some more food and something to drink, she thought. Janet grabbed a fresh bottle of water and quickly chugged down half of it. Oh, and look, goodie.... Lunchables again. She ate the portion of protein from the package first and then moved on to eat the other items in the prepackaged lunch. Still hungry, Janet spied her half bagel that she hadn't eaten earlier. It was still wrapped securely as far as she could tell in the sandwich bag. It was a little crushed, but food was food. She grabbed the bagel and greedily finished that off too. She took a few more swallows of water and then leaned back against the wall to rest. Feeling marginally better after the food, Janet knew she now had some serious thinking to do.

Soon it would be night again. She didn't want to let David know she was now was able to walk again; he definitely didn't need to know that she had regained some of her strength. But, even though she was stronger, Janet knew she was still a train wreck. She could feel the swelling on her face and was sure it was bruised black and blue and that she looked battered. Okay Janet, she thought to herself, what was the plan?

She hoped Kelly would bring some more food before nighttime returned. That would be her best opportunity to escape. She needed to let Kelly see her face, see what damage her monster of a husband had done to her, perhaps making Kelly find some spark of humanity still left inside of her. Janet figured she would just have to make it up as she went along. She really wasn't in any situation to guess or predict what would happen next. Her ability to control her life had been taken completely away. Janet sighed and leaned back, gently resting her bruised head against the well. She closed her eyes and just decided to wait.

CHAPTER 13

The sound of the trapdoor, creakily opening up, woke Janet with a start and she quickly looked over to where David was sleeping. His eyes, unfortunately, had also opened up at the noise. Crap, the door had woken him up, too.

"Hey David, loser of a husband... come over here. And bring your girlfriend with you. I'm not taking any more of your stupid excuses why she hasn't been awake for meals. And hurry up about it, before I lose my patience and decide not to feed you." Kelly sounded really pissed off and seemed very serious that there would be no food until she saw Janet.

David looked at Janet and said, "Well I guess we better do what she says." David put his hands up to his head and raked his fingers through his oily mess of hair. Then, after shaking his hair as if he were on a photo shoot or something, like that would make it all better, he stood up and started walking over to the trapdoor. "Are you coming?" he asked Janet.

"I can't get up by myself. I just feel so tired and weak; could you please help me up?" Janet had somehow mustered up acting skills she didn't know she had. David smiled and came over, he seemed happy to see that she needed his help, and he slowly lifted Janet to her feet.

"Do you want me to help you walk over there?" David looked at Janet with a concerned face. Apparently, he enjoyed playing rescuer. Janet nodded her head yes, and then leaned her body heavily against him and put her arm over his shoulder to further "enhance" her extreme dependence on him. Then they both moved the few steps together toward the trapdoor.

"Well, finally, Sleeping Beauty decides to show her pretty face," Kelly remarked sarcastically. But then, after seeing the condition of Janet's face, Kelly's demeanor changed somewhat.

"Huh. For some reason, your girlfriend's pretty face doesn't look so pretty now. Hard night of partying, huh? Hey Janet, did you fall down drunk and land on your face in a drunken stupor?" Kelly scoffed and shook her head. "Janet, ya gotta learn how to carry your alcohol! Something you will learn. But I'm thinking not tonight, that just may be too soon. After all, I don't want to spoil you two too much." Kelly stepped away from the trapdoor for a few moments and Janet could hear her moving some things overhead.

"You're lucky today. Homemade sandwiches. I make a hell of a sandwich. Now David, I know he could live on ham sandwiches. But I figured I would give Janet a choice of what sort of processed meat she wanted. Let's see, we have ham, bologna, and turkey. Well, Miss Janet, what flavor of sandwich would you like?"

Janet thought for a second and replied, "Ham would be fine. Thank you, Kelly, for asking." Janet tried to sound as tired and weak as she could, but it really wasn't that hard to fake. Kelly had seen her face, and she couldn't really believe that Janet had gotten all these bumps and bruises from falling down, could she? Maybe Janet had seriously misjudged Kelly; maybe Kelly had stopped remembering how to be human.

"Okay, just a second while I slap some lunchmeat into your sandwich, Janet. Whoops, you accidentally got two slices. Guess that makes it your lucky day. Watch out below, incoming." Kelly indelicately dropped the two sandwiches down to the cement floor near Janet's feet. Thankfully, she had sealed the sandwiches in plastic zip bags, and they both fell to the floor intact. "And here is your water." Again, Kelly dropped the two water bottles, both of them hitting the floor with a thud. But this time, one of the plastic bottles had split a bit with the impact and water started leaking out of it on to the floor. "Crap." Kelly said. "Was wondering when that would happen. Luckily I always bring spares." Kelly dropped down another water bottle, which this time luckily didn't break.

David hurriedly reached out and picked up the water bottle that had split and, seeing that there was no way to stop the liquid from eventually emptying out, he held the bottle over his mouth and drank the bit that was left. "Didn't want to waste it," he said to no one in particular. Janet had slowly started to reach down to pick up the sandwiches, trying to make a production about how weak she was. As if that mattered now, since neither Kelly nor David seemed to have any sort of compassion left in them.

David quickly grabbed both the sandwiches before Janet could touch them. After a quick examination, he kept the one with two pieces of ham for himself and then handed the other one off to Janet. "Dibs!" he said and laughed. What a complete and utter jerk, Janet thought to herself and then she made her way over to their "dining room" to eat.

All in all, the sandwich was really good. It had real mayonnaise on it, just the way Janet liked it. Of course, the mayonnaise was a problem for David. "Spiteful witch. She knows I don't like mayo," David said as he shoved the last bits of food into his mouth. "I'm still hungry." David said eyeing Janet's sandwich. Janet turned her body away from him to guard her sandwich and sped up her eating. There was no way he was getting her food from her, no way.

David shrugged, pretending that he didn't want the other sandwich in the first place, and then made a big deal about getting up and stretching.

"I don't know about you, but I am going stir crazy in this hellhole. I need some exercise. Since I obviously would have to wait a long time in here to be able to use the exercise bike, I guess I will have to make do." David got down on the floor and started doing pushups. Apparently, David didn't work out as much as he pretended he did, because after about eight of them he already looked like he was starting to strain. "Boring," David said, trying to cover up the fact that he wasn't so good in the upper torso department by quickly switching to stretching exercises and then finally to just walking back and forth in the room, all the while making such a big production number out of it that Janet kind of almost felt pity for him, *almost*. He was way out of shape.

After David had done about 20 laps back and forth across the room, he sat down on the ground, trying hard to stifle his heavy breathing from the exertion. He then stretched, yawned, and said, "Oh my god, I am so sleepy. I think that quick nap I had before chow just wasn't enough. Okay, here is a bad news and good news thing. Bad news, we are stuck in a hole. Good news, I'm finally catching up on my sleep." That last sentence he trailed off, as once again with his head on the ground, he had quickly fallen to sleep.

Funny, Janet thought, I don't feel sleepy at all. She felt so much more clearheaded after eating the sandwich and drinking some more water. The good news, Janet thought to herself, is that I'm probably losing those few extra pounds that don't ever seem to want to go away.

With her energy renewed, Janet got up and started to pace the room again. With David sleeping, Janet had an opportunity to increase her walking endurance. This time she did about 15 laps of the room, a piddly amount really, but she hadn't had to use the wall for balance. Then, after the laps, Janet lay down on the floor and tried to do some stretching. What was the name of that yoga thing, downward dog or something? Janet thought she kind of remembered what that was from the class she had taken, did that, and then started to try different ways to stretch some of the kinks out of her back.

Suddenly, Janet thought she heard movement overhead. As she looked up, she saw that Kelly was slowly opening the trapdoor, trying to do so as quietly as she could. Janet looked at Kelly with confusion, and then Kelly put her finger up to her lips... she wanted Janet to be quiet. Janet nodded her head yes, to let Kelly know she understood. When the door was completely open, Kelly put her two hands together and laid her head on them, then closed her eyes and acted as if she was sleeping. After she did that movement, she pointed at David. She must want to know if David was sleeping. Janet nodded her head yes. Kelly motioned Janet away from the area under the trapdoor and then slowly lowered the ladder down until it firmly stood on the floor.

Janet watched the ladder descending, not believing her eyes. Oh my god, was she finally getting out of here? Before Janet could even take a step toward the ladder, Kelly was down it, standing on the floor next to her, gesturing for Janet to go up the ladder ahead of her. She didn't have to ask Janet twice. Janet quickly started up the ladder, but she realized after the first few rungs that, although she felt better, the climb was a little more difficult and therefore not as fast as she thought it would be. Kelly had already started up the ladder after her.

All of a sudden, while she was concentrating hard on moving up the ladder, Janet heard a commotion below her. David had apparently woken up—if he had ever really been asleep—and had crossed the room and just as quickly, he grabbed Kelly by the waist and threw her to the ground. David then grabbed the ladder with both hands and yanked on it, shaking it as hard as he could. Janet lost her grip. She just couldn't hold on in her weakened state. Her hands slipped off the rung she was on and she slowly slid down the ladder to the floor.

Meanwhile, Kelly had gotten back up; she walked over to David and kicked him as hard as she could in the back of his leg. David turned to retaliate and, as Kelly fumbled in her coat pocket, David pulled his hand back and punched Kelly hard, right in the middle of her face. Kelly hit the floor.

David whipped around, looked at Janet, and growled menacingly with his fist raised. "Are you next?" he asked. Janet quickly backed away from David's reach, and then shook her head no. At that, David quickly scrambled up the ladder and then with seeming ease pulled the ladder up and out of the hole. Janet heard screaming, a loud "Woot!" David was obviously celebrating his freedom and—as he looked down at Kelly and Janet—he also began to celebrate his incredible luck at snaring them both down in the hole together.

"See you later, bitches!" David laughed and dropped the trapdoor closed. Janet couldn't believe the change in events. She had missed her chance at escape. She started to cry.

CHAPTER 14

Janet felt broken. She had gotten her opportunity and she had missed it. Actually, it had been stolen from her. By David. She had been so stupid, so stupid to have ever trusted him. This is what I get for always trying to find the good in people, she thought. Some people obviously just don't have any good inside them to find. Janet wiped her eyes and, grabbing a couple of squares of toilet paper, blew her nose. After having come so close to finally climbing out of this little piece of hell and back into the world, having that freedom snatched away from her at the last second was almost more than Janet could take.

"I am so sorry," Kelly quietly said from across the room. Her voice sounded distorted, probably because she had her head tilted back and her nose pinched closed with two fingers, as she tried to stop the stream of blood that was pouring from her nose. Already the front of her shirt was covered in the dark red liquid. "I'm so sorry, Janet."

Janet's first impulse was to scream like a banshee, run over there, and kick Kelly until her foot hurt. Then she would switch feet. But, that stupid thing inside of her, what was it called—humanity—reared its ugly head. Janet sighed. She silently unrolled a wad of toilet paper from the roll, walked across the room, and with a blank face held it out for Kelly to grab.

Kelly saw the toilet paper, leaned over, took it from Janet's hand, and then pressed it up against her bleeding nose. "Thanks," she said.

"You betcha! Anything else you would like? I'm sorry I don't have much to offer you. Oh wait, I have nothing to offer you. Since you are the sole reason I am down in this fucking hole in the ground in the first place… have I thanked you yet for that?" Janet sarcastically asked Kelly.

Kelly ripped off pieces of the toilet paper, rolled them up, and stuffed the two tissue rolls up her nose, each into a nostril. Then, trying to compose herself, Kelly took a few futile swipes at trying to clean up her face. David had really hit her hard.

Janet watched as the whole toilet paper process took place, watching as Kelly carefully rolled the two pieces of tissue and then jammed them up into her nose. She looked at the quasi-comical scene of Kelly sitting on the floor with the toilet paper sticking out of her nose, with muck smeared across her face, and Janet just couldn't help herself. She started laughing. She was laughing because the whole situation was so absurd, that she now was stuck down in the dirt hole with the person who had kidnapped her and who had kept her hostage here in the first place. Janet laughed until she could barely breathe and until tears started running down her face. After a short time, Janet finally stopped laughing, but the stress relief had been great. She needed to see some humor, somewhere in this stupid mess. After she had calmed down and no more laughter was left in her, she sighed and sat on the floor beside Kelly.

Kelly looked over at Janet and shook her head from side to side. "Okay, that was the last response I expected. I fully expected to be beaten to a bloody pulp for doing what I did to you. I wish I could travel back in time and take it all back. The whole stupid situation, which in some crazy anger-induced dreamland that I was in seemed at the time like a rational idea, just all of a sudden seemed to get out of hand and way too real. When I looked down at you, and saw what that monster had done to your face, I snapped back into the ugly reality of what I had done to you. I knew... I just knew I couldn't do this to you anymore. You must think I am a horrible human being."

Kelly stopped talking then, as the toilet paper in her nose was already soaked and dripping blood down again onto her shirt. She took the remaining bit of toilet paper she had left and replaced the bloody ones in her nose. The flow of blood seemed to be slowing down a bit.

"Well, I've got to tell you. My first instinct a few minutes ago was to kick the shit out of you. But, again, I am too nice and you looked so awful with that blood running down your face, I knew I just couldn't do that to you. That isn't the first time he's hit you, is it?" Janet grabbed for the toilet paper and handed a few more sheets to Kelly.

"Um, no... definitely not the first time he has ever hit me. But it will be his last. I can guarantee you that. He will never hurt me or another woman ever again." Kelly's eyes were burning with hate. The hate in Kelly's eyes was so intense, so white hot that it was hard for Janet to even look at her.

"Okay, I understand that feeling. But maybe you didn't notice that David is up there and we are down here. I'm sure by this time he has jumped in my car and driven like a bat out of hell down the road, without a second thought about letting us rot to death down here." Again, Janet just couldn't believe her luck. She had just been so close to getting out of here.

"No, I don't think he will drive off and leave us here, unless he has suddenly acquired the skill of hotwiring a car. Silly David, I have the keys to your car, safely hidden." Kelly managed a smile. Her face was already swelling and starting to bruise up.

"Oh, thank God. Finally, something good happens. But couldn't he just walk to the nearest road or something and hitch a ride? What's to stop him?" Janet thought about what it would be like, how hard it would be to die of hunger and thirst. Really, it was not the way she wanted to have to leave this world.

"Oh, I know David. He won't leave. He has two women trapped in a storm shelter, or whatever this hole in the ground was intended to be. He would never miss the fun of having two captive women all to himself and totally dependent on him, and then feeling like he has free reign to do whatever sick things he wants to do to us. Trust me, he is a sadistic son of a bitch" Kelly said vehemently. Janet knew Kelly was right; David wasn't about to leave without having "fun" first.

"Okay then, what's your plan? Because I'm all out of them. There's no way we're getting out of here, unless a magic ladder falls from the sky and saves us." Janet closed her eyes and rubbed them hard, as if by rubbing them she could wake up from this nightmare. Janet was almost at her limit. She couldn't take much more.

"I don't have a plan... yet. But I do have this." Kelly reached into her pocket and pulled out the Taser. "Oh, and gum... I have gum. Want some?" Kelly held out an unopened package of Wrigley's spearmint gum toward Janet.

Janet smiled and then laughed like a little girl. "Oh my god, you have gum. Yes, please... gum. My mouth and teeth feel disgusting." Janet reached for the gum and quickly opened the package and pulled out two pieces. "One for you?" Janet asked Kelly. Kelly smiled and took the piece of gum from Janet's hand. They both unwrapped their gum and stuck it in their mouths, and for a time, they seemed content just being able to enjoy the simple normality of chewing gum.

After a few minutes, Janet finally broke the silence. "Okay, now we have a weapon. Oh, and gum. Now if we were MacGyver we could use just those two things to come up with a way to blast our way out of here, save ourselves, and probably save some kittens from a well for good measure. I'm not feeling very MacGyver-y at the moment. How about you?"

Kelly sat for a moment longer, chewing loudly and cracking her gum before answering. "Well, I do know one thing... he will be back for us. We are his weakness. Actually, in some ways, we have more power over him than he does over us."

"How the hell is that?" Janet looked at Kelly as if she was crazy, and then Janet realized that Kelly probably already knew that she was.

"We are David's dream come true. Two women, trapped in a hole, and he is the only one who knows. And knowing his sick mind, David is probably already conjuring up a sadistic threesome. Which, of course, would include him doing a lot of punching and God knows what else to us." Kelly said remorsefully. "But we can use that to our advantage. Women have the ultimate weapon over men in a way: they have their sexuality. David would never miss the chance to dominate two women totally, slowly raping and torturing us to death. That is how he gets off, that is how he makes himself a 'real man.' He is a sick, sick person."

Kelly looked toward Janet… and in her eyes, Janet could see a new kind of cold gleam take over, replacing the almost frightened look she had seen earlier. Kelly had retaken her power back. She looked more determined than ever to get back at David, no matter what the cost.

Janet let that bit of information and the look in Kelly's eyes sink in. The thought of that bastard touching her again, with the depravity she now knew was inside of him, repulsed her. He was never going to touch her, ever again. She knew now she would die before she ever let him touch her again. Of that, she was sure.

After a few minutes, as Janet's conviction that she did not want to go out of the world as a victim had grown, she began to feel that something like a shared kindred spirit had grown between the two of them. Janet had a ton of questions she wanted—no, needed—to ask Kelly, things that she needed to know. Along with that, Janet had some of her own horror at the hands of David to share with Kelly. Janet didn't look forward to reliving that last part, having to share with Kelly things that she wished she could always and forever wall off in a safe place in her brain. But Janet realized inside that she needed to let it out; she refused to allow herself to be a victim anymore.

"Okay, here come the million questions. And please, please answer them honestly. I just can't take being lied to anymore, do you understand me?" Janet looked at Kelly. Kelly nodded her head yes, and then the grim look returned to her face.

Janet started. "Okay, first up, why the hell did you marry that monster? You must have known he had a dark...evil... side."

Kelly sighed; she just seemed so incredibly tired. "David wasn't always like that. He was so good to me. I had had a rough life. Shortly before I met David, both of my parents had died in a car accident. All of a sudden I was all alone in the world. David seemed like my savior. He let me cry on his shoulder, talk until I was hoarse, and gave me the space to grieve that I so desperately needed. David knew I was now alone in the world, and I believe he used my aloneness to his advantage. We had only been together for two months before he asked me to marry him. I said yes... I was so lonely. I missed my parents so much; they had always been there for me and now they were both gone. David and I got married exactly three months after we had first met. And happily, in the beginning, we started to make a life together. But then things started to change."

Kelly paused for a few moments and Janet took that opportunity to speak. "I can't imagine marrying someone after just three months. But then, I didn't just lose both my parents at the same time in a car accident. So I guess I am in no place to judge." She did begin to feel sorry for Kelly; it must have been so hard on her to lose both parents. "So how did things start to change?"

"I was finishing up nursing school, so I had to spend a lot of time studying and getting ready for finals. David wasn't happy about this, he eventually told me. He thought a wife should spend more time with her husband, not spending time with strangers until late in the night studying at the library. Before we were married, all of that was okay with him. The school and classes, the studying, the friends, the staying out late at the library, was never an issue. That was until we got married; then, all of a sudden, I wasn't just an individual any more, I was a wife. His wife. He had strange and archaic rules about how a wife should be, and every day there seemed to be more and more rules. I did everything I could to please him, but he still got mad... and made sure I knew. He always looked sullen and pouted all the time. He didn't seem like the same person I married."

Kelly stopped the story and turned to Janet. "I should have gotten out then. But, typical female, I thought I could change him. Why do women think that this is even possible? Have you ever seen even one example of it working? I haven't. I guess we all see what we want to see."

Janet, at this point, started to feel genuinely sorry for Kelly. She had seen many women go into a relationship or a marriage thinking, "Gee whiz, he will change for me." It didn't work. In fact, it never worked.

"So, after putting up with these rules and the anger and the stupid jealousy, I finally told him to knock it off. I told him that he knew what my life was about before he married me. That was the first time he hit me."

Kelly sighed, shook her head, and continued. "Of course, after he hit me, he was all contrite... went on and on that he was a bad husband, his life was just tough right now, he couldn't believe he hit the woman he loved with his whole 'heart and soul.' He apologized in every way he could think of. Bought me flowers, took me out to eat at fancy restaurants, bought me jewelry. I really believed he hadn't meant to do it— that he was just stressed by other things going on in his life. So I forgave him and we moved on from there."

Janet knew she had to stop Kelly at that point. "If a man ever hit me, my husband for instance, I would be out the door so fast. And I would never look back. Never."

Kelly kind of sadly smiled and nodded her head. "See, I used to think that too. No man was ever going to hit me. But he was so convincing about being sorry and he was so overly nice to me for so long, I thought it would never happen again. Plus, I really had nowhere else to go. School had taken up most of my time over the last few years, and any free time I had I spent with my Mom and my Dad. But since they were taken away, I didn't have anyone. I had no one to turn to, nowhere to go. I didn't think at the time I was trapped... but I was."

Kelly stopped and looked at Janet. "You wouldn't happen to have any water left, would you? I hate to ask, but my throat hurts so much."

Janet reached for her bottle and handed it to Kelly. "Just take a couple of sips. That might be the last water we ever get." Kelly took a couple of quick drinks and handed the bottle back to Janet with a quiet thank you. Then, she cleared her throat and went back to her story.

"About that time, David started to drink. He had always told me when we were dating and stuff, that he didn't drink... never had, never would. That was fine with me; I was no big drinker myself. But apparently, he had a 'problem with alcohol,' which was why he didn't drink. He had gotten a DUI and a charge of resisting arrest, I later found out. That was the only reason why he didn't drink, at least in front of me.

"At first he pretended he wasn't drinking; he probably stopped at a bar on the way home from someplace. I pretended I didn't smell the alcohol on his breath. Then, one day, he came home with a big bottle of whiskey, plopped it on the kitchen counter and said, 'Let's have a party! I all of a sudden want a drink.' So, I had a couple of drinks with him. I was kind of relieved that his drinking was out in the open now. I don't like secrets between couples."

Janet nodded her head in agreement. She knew that at some point soon, she would have to tell Kelly what her sick, evil husband had done to her the other night, but right now didn't seem like the time.

"David was an ugly drunk, which I absolutely knew when I sent down that alcohol to you two. I am so sorry for having anything to do with providing him access to alcohol. I guess my brain thought—I don't know... I was so confused— 'Awww, he won't hurt her, she isn't his wife.' Guess I was wrong about that."

Janet touched her face and then moved her hand toward the back of her head. Both places still hurt a great deal. She tried to push the injuries out of her mind, because thinking about them just brought back the other thoughts. And she didn't want to have those.

"He started to hit me more and more often," Kelly went on. "I had forgotten to pick up ketchup on the way home. Or I didn't return his call right away. He was sure in his mind I was cheating, but I wasn't, at that point. I was just trying to get through my days and my nights. And then one night, when he was really, really drunk ... I refused to have sex with him. That really set him off. He hit me and then hit me again in the face. He ripped off my clothes and forced himself on me sexually. I guess in retrospect, he had raped me. The next morning, I was beaten, bruised, and hurting, both physically and emotionally. I couldn't believe he had done that to me.

"David pretended nothing out of the ordinary had happened the night before. 'We had some fun,' according to him. It was fun? Really? Because it definitely wasn't fun for me. I had to go to work the next day at the hospital. My face was nowhere near beginning to heal; actually, it looked worse and worse throughout the day, but I still had to work, or my career could have been in jeopardy... I don't know. So I went to the hospital and laughingly told everyone the story of how David and I had been hiking... and clumsy me had slipped off the path, and tumbled down a little way, hitting my head on rocks on the way down. I think everyone believed me, or pretended to. Except for Kevin."

"Finally, we get to Kevin. You did have an affair with him, right?" Janet felt no qualms about asking her that question. Kelly owed it to her to tell her the truth. Janet felt she wanted and definitely needed to know everything—why all of this bad stuff was happening to her.

"Well, it wasn't an affair at first, at least for a long time. Kevin was just another nice guy, a sympathetic listener. From the first day he saw the bruises on my face, he had refused to believe my story about me falling off the hiking trail. He said he knew what had really happened. He said he had a sister who had stayed with an abusive husband for far too long." Kelly directed her next comment directly to Janet. "Janet, he was so nice to me. I could tell Kevin was a decent and honest person. We became fast friends. Just friends, you know? But best friends."

Janet had in the past and still had friends like that in her life. She knew what a comfort it was to have someone you could talk to, confide in. Her real friends had and would always be an important part of her life, so she knew what Kelly was talking about.

"So... where was I? Oh yeah. At about that time, David started coming home later and later at night, which frankly was fine by me. I never liked to be around him when he had been drinking, for obvious reasons. I knew he was cheating on me, but by then I had gotten to the point where I didn't care. It took some of the pressure off of me. Still, some nights, he would come home and he would physically force me to have sex with him. I would fight back, but that would only make it worse... I would wake up bleeding from where he had forced himself into my body. So I decided to stop fighting. And... that actually made him madder yet."

"Wow. I think he did say you were frigid or something toward the end of your relationship. Yeah, right. I would have done the exact same thing you did, I guess, if I had been in your shoes." Janet trailed off and looked out into space. She looked extremely sad.

Kelly took this as a sign that maybe Janet actually understood why she had done what she had done to her. But that wasn't everything. She wanted Janet to know everything; actually, she needed to know everything. So Kelly knew she had to continue.

"One day, apparently to kill some time on his lunch break, David stopped by the hospital to have lunch with me, or probably just to check up on me, really. He saw Kevin and me walking out of the hospital I guess, and then together over to a café that was a favorite with the hospital staff, so he automatically assumed I was having an affair with Kevin, which I wasn't. That night, he beat the living hell out of me. Screamed at me, calling me a whore and a slut and all sorts of nasty things and he accused me of doing even more horrible things—things I didn't even know existed. He kept asking me, 'Who is that guy I saw you with today? Were you fucking him? How many people are you fucking?'

"His questions started to get crazier and crazier by the minute. He finally hit me so hard he knocked me out. And he apparently forced himself on me again that night, while I was unconscious and near comatose from the beating... because the next morning I hurt so much, and was bleeding so much -- I was scared out of my mind. I knew what had happened... and I also knew what could have happened. I guess at about that time, I started to think he probably would actually try to kill me at some point. I didn't know how far he would go; I had become that scared."

Janet knew that this was the point where she should share her story about David with Kelly. But Janet just couldn't. She didn't want to think about it, talk about it, and have to relive it in her mind. Here David had done the same thing to his own wife, who he claimed to love with all his heart and soul. Janet just couldn't, she just couldn't say a thing.

Kelly got up and stretched and walked around for a little while. "My butt is asleep. It is really, really uncomfortable on that floor." She looked over at Janet and said, "Oh, you already know that."

"Um, yeah." Janet said. "This cement floor and I have become very acquainted with each other." Janet watched as Kelly walked around the room for a bit, stretched, yawned, and then sat down next to her to continue her story.

"I couldn't go to work the next day. There was simply no way of explaining the condition I was in, to Kevin or to anybody, so I stayed at home. For three days I stayed at home, until the hospital finally called me and said my job was at risk unless I came back in. So I did. Kevin took one look at me and he put his arms around me and held me tight. I cried and cried in his arms. People were walking by and saw us, but I didn't care. Neither of us cared. Kevin told me I needed to talk to the police this time. But I refused to. I didn't want the scandal of it all to come out, and then become the subject of conversation for everybody to talk about for the next couple of weeks, or months, or for however long. Part of me inside knew David would somehow get away scot-free, so I didn't tell the police. And I didn't think twice about taking Kevin up on his offer of his guest bedroom for the night. I was in no way going back to my house to face more of the same."

Kelly looked at Janet and said, "See, I wasn't cheating on David then. For one thing, how could I? I was so torn and bruised I didn't want anyone touching me. But after a couple of weeks of staying at Kevin's house, we finally realized that our feelings for each other were more than just friendship. So one night, we finally slept together. It was the most magical night of my life. I was where I knew I should be."

Kelly's eyes started tearing up, but she seemed determined to finish her story without crying. "In retrospect, I should have known. I should have known David would follow us to Kevin's house, find out where he, and now I, lived. I never should have put Kevin in that situation. But, I loved Kevin. And he loved me. And that made me feel safe."

Janet looked at Kelly and could see a wave of sadness wash over her face. While she was talking about Kevin, Kelly's face came alive and she saw a side of her she had never seen before... a peaceful, loving, happy side. Then instantly, the look on her face changed again when she turned back to the subject of David. It truly looked to Janet like a wave had come and washed all the happiness away. Kelly looked numb.

"One night, Kevin was working a different shift than I was. And at the time I expected him to usually be home, he didn't show up. I was scared, thought he had gotten in a car wreck or something. I asked around at the hospital and people who had seen Kevin the day he disappeared said that Kevin had seemed like nothing was out of the ordinary. I checked with his parents and his sister. They hadn't heard from him either. And the fact that I was so frantic, crying and quizzing them on the phone, made them concerned too. We drove back and forth along the roads we thought Kevin would have taken on the way home from the hospital. Then we tried alternate routes, always stopping and getting out of the car and looking over the side of the road to if we could see his car or something. We finally told the police. They were sympathetic, but they really didn't have anything to go on. Kevin was an adult; maybe he had gotten sick of his life and just decided to disappear."

Kelly stopped there and looked toward Janet. "I knew that Kevin would never do that to me. We cared so much about each other when we were just friends, and now we were both friends and lovers. And he never would have left his parents and his sister without letting them know he was at least okay. He doted on them... they were truly a family who were there for each other. We all knew something had happened to him. An accident or a mugging or something and that he was probably dead. But I knew. I *knew*, Janet. I knew deep down in my heart that David had killed him. I just knew it."

Janet just couldn't believe what she was hearing. Such a wildly different story than the one David had told her. That Kelly was frigid; that Kelly started cheating on him first and that she had moved out when finally, just for payback, David cheated on her. Janet knew without a doubt that Kelly was telling the truth, that David had killed Kevin. He had killed him and stashed his body somewhere, a place where probably nobody would ever find him.

Janet did what anyone would do when they heard that someone they knew had had someone close to them die. She put her arms around Kelly, and when she did, Kelly finally at last started crying. She cried and she cried. It was like all the grief was coming out of her at once. Janet just held her close. They both lay down on the floor beside each other. Janet pulled the blanket over them both and then Janet held Kelly in her arms -- trying to comfort her. Kelly cried until she had just finally cried herself to sleep. Shortly after that, Janet fell asleep too.

CHAPTER 15

Janet and Kelly were rudely awakened to the sound of David's voice. "Hot damn, we got a little girl-on-girl action happening over here. Wifey, I always thought you were probably the kind of girl who could go both ways. I guess I was right."

"Just… shut up," Kelly said as she rose to her feet and, after a brief stretch, tried to wipe the sleep from her eyes. "You don't get to make any comments on who or what I sleep with."

"We are still married, aren't we, Kelly? That's what this is all about, kidnapping me, so I would come back into your life again? But that doesn't explain Janet; she was just an innocent bystander." Turning his attention toward Janet, David said in a lewd voice, "Or at least she was, right Janet?"

Janet pretended she hadn't heard him. Even just hearing David's voice made her skin crawl. She slowly stood up and stood next to Kelly, but did not make eye contact with her. Janet had no idea how to play this situation. Should she act like she still sided with David… or should she let David know that she knew the truth about him, that he was a murderer… oh, and a sicko rapist? Luckily for Janet at that moment, she didn't have to decide.

"Well, let's see. We've changed roles, which means that now I am the jail keeper. And according to state law, I have to feed you. So, let's see what I got here." David ducked away from the opening for a second before continuing, "Oh, and by the way Kelly, nice house you got up there, almost a step up from living in a barn. No electricity, oh... and yeah, your generator is just about out of gas, there is no running water, and an outhouse? For Christ's sake, Kelly! Why in God's name would you choose to live like a pig?"

Kelly looked up at David. If looks could kill, David would be dead meat on a stick. "Well, not like I am rolling in money or anything. Just cut the crap David, are you going to give us food and water or what?"

David laughed. "Well, I must say that since you left our marriage to go off and sleep with all the lowlifes, you sure grew a couple. And since you asked so nicely, you each get... ta-dahh! A bottle of water and an apple." David dropped the food and water to the floor below, not caring whom or what the food hit and whether it would survive the fall. "I think I'm going to enjoy keeping my new pets, although it is going to get pretty hard to feed you pretty soon unless I stock up at a grocery store. Which reminds me Kelly, you wouldn't by the way happen to have the car keys?"

"Oh these keys, you mean?" Kelly said mockingly as she took the keys out of her pocket and jangled them in the air. "Yeah, I have them. Why don't you come on down here and try to get them from me, David? "

David looked down at Kelly and then at Janet and shook his head. "Okay, have it your way." David dropped the hatch down with a loud bang and he was gone.

"Nice guy you got yourself there, Kelly. Why the heck did you mock him with the keys? That is just going to piss him off more." Janet said, looking a little annoyed. Janet and Kelly went about retrieving their food, each picking up a nearly smashed apple and a bottle of water.

"That's the idea." Kelly said. Then with one of her hands, she stopped Janet from taking a bite of her apple. "When I threw those ham sandwiches down here to you, I deliberately gave you two pieces of ham, because I knew David would claim it as his own. And so I had put a little sleeping medicine in that one."

"Oh," Janet said as she remembered the failed rescue attempt. "Well then, why did he wake up"?

"I have no idea." Kelly said. "It should have knocked him out for a couple of hours, or I never would have come down here to get you. The bad thing is, the sleeping medicine is up there with him, in the house. He is bound to find it sooner or later and then try somehow to lace our food with it. So, here is what I think we should do. We each take turns being the first to eat. If the first one to eat doesn't fall to sleep after I'd say, about twenty minutes, then the other person can eat. We can't let him get us trapped down here while we're both drugged with sleep medicine at the same time. That would be a very, very bad thing."

Janet's eyes got huge at that thought. "This just keeps getting better and better. Well, I vote I eat first… mostly because I am starving and I really wouldn't mind being able to sleep with you babysitting me."

Kelly agreed and they both lay down on the cement floor to eat. Janet quickly ate her apple… the whole thing, seeds and all. Then she opened her water bottle. "It seems like it's still factory sealed. I don't think he could get something into a sealed bottle without us noticing, do you?"

"Um, doubt it." Kelly agreed and after Janet was done, they both sat there on the hard floor and waited the twenty minutes to see if Janet's food had been drugged. Luckily, Kelly had a watch so they didn't have to guesstimate. Neither of them wanted to screw up.

During those twenty minutes, Kelly gave Janet some instructions. "Okay, the Taser." She took the thing out of her pocket and showed Janet how to work it. After a few brief instructions on how to aim and shoot the thing, Kelly was satisfied that Janet could protect them if need be. "So," Kelly continued... "If I got the drugged food and am knocked out after eating it, I want you to take the Taser and hide it somewhere out of sight but where you will still have quick access to it. Then, you have to lie down and pretend to be knocked out by the sleeping medicine too, so it looks like we shared our food or something. He is going to try to sedate us both at the same time, so he would expect to see us both unconscious before he would dare to come down the ladder. When he gets close enough and you are sure you will be successful, shoot him with as much voltage as you can. Don't hesitate. We might only get one chance with that gun."

Janet agreed to the plan, then sat and watched as Kelly ate her apple and drank some of her water from the bottle. Twenty minutes later, Kelly seemed fine too, so they figured David hadn't thought, or didn't know a way, to put the sleeping medicine into the apples. After a few minutes of quiet, with both of them staring out into space, both still hungry and thirsty, they finally started to talk again.

"So, why kidnap me too? You didn't need me. I mean seriously, why?" Janet finally asked Kelly. This, for Janet, was one of the harder questions for her to ask, because she was afraid of what she might hear. Nevertheless, Janet felt like she really needed to ask it, not only for her own peace of mind but also for her safety. Janet felt safe with Kelly now, but she couldn't help but remember how at one point she had felt safe with David too.

"My plan had never been to grab anyone else. Just David." Kelly began. "But the day I had planned on for taking him hostage, I had to change my plan when you showed up at the Starbucks and met with him. At first, I had only planned on just grabbing him, scaring the crap out of him, and then beating him until he talked. Then when I saw you, my initial plan seemed stupid and dangerous. I really wasn't sure that David would ever tell me the truth about Kevin, no matter what I did to him. Then I thought if he got drunk... really drunk... he might just brag about it to another woman, to impress her or something. I didn't know you two didn't know each other and that you had really just met. I thought you were dating or something. I thought he might, I don't know, at least give you some clue or something about what he had done to Kevin. Or maybe even just tell you where he had dumped Kevin's body."

Kelly paused for a moment; there was obvious pain in her eyes. "I even foolishly thought I might be doing you a favor by letting you know what you were getting in to with him if you continued to date him. So, I changed the plan."

"Okay, well that might make sense to you, but it makes no sense to me." Janet struggled to think how best to put the words together so Kelly could understand her failed logic.

"But then why did you give him the alcohol? If you knew he was violent when he was drunk, didn't you think about or even care about that after he got very drunk, he would probably beat me up too? And then rape me?" The last part barely came out as a whisper from Janet's mouth.

Kelly sat across from Janet, and just stared at her, as the reality of what she had let happen to Janet finally sank in. With real pain in her eyes, Kelly asked Janet the question she already knew the answer to, "He raped you?"

"Yes, he raped me." Janet said. Once those words were out of her mouth, she felt as though a brick wall she had built in her brain was smashed open and that at last she could finally express the feelings and emotions she really wanted to express to Kelly. "He hit me and he yelled at me, he humiliated me, and then he finally beat my head against the floor until I was unconscious. And then he raped me. When I was most helpless and vulnerable, I could have been dead for all he cared... he raped me ... violently. So was that part of your little plan, Kelly?"

Kelly looked like her face had simply caved in. She couldn't meet Janet's eyes, and instead she closed her eyes and then just sat in silence for a while. Janet sat there too, watching and waiting for her, waiting for an answer that she desperately needed to hear.

Kelly talked very softly at first. "Janet, I never in a million years would have thought that this would happen to you... that he would rape you. I thought just possibly, at the most he would yell at you and call you names, maybe, I don't know, maybe even slap you. But after all that, I figured David would then get all contrite and apologize. I mean, he was with other women after me, or probably even while we were still together. I think if he had raped someone else during that time, if he had done to some other woman what he had done to me, I would think somebody would have reported it and then the cops would have shown up at our door. I really thought you would be okay. I thought David only raped me because I was something he owned, a thing.... I was his wife. I didn't think he would rape you. Janet... I am so sorry. I know you will never be able to forgive me for this, but never in a million years would I wish on my worst enemy the abuse David subjected me to over the time we were married. Oh, god... I've screwed up everything."

Kelly looked like she was going to cry, but for some reason she didn't. Janet noticed that Kelly's eyes had glazed over and they now had kind of a vacant look to them. To Janet it seemed, a part of Kelly had had gone away.

"Well, he did rape me, Kelly. And because of what you did, you are partially responsible for it. I can't blame you for all of it, but you definitely loaded the gun and gave it to an alcoholic person with violent tendencies. David did the raping, not you, but you knew how he was. You should have known what might happen."

Janet could just feel the anger building in waves in her body, some waves growing bigger by the minute, and others receding and then starting to rebuild themselves again. Getting this out, telling this absolutely horrifying and barbaric thing to Kelly that her husband, David, had done to her, finally letting Kelly know she was to blame for what had happened to her, made Janet feel stronger and better. Maybe, what were the words they used to express it? Janet felt empowered by releasing some of her rage and anger that had built up and was blackening her soul.

Kelly just sat there, quietly staring into space, but Janet knew that Kelly had heard her. Kelly had flinched whenever Janet said the word rape and more so when she had said that she, Kelly, was partially responsible. Janet sat back and closed her eyes too. She felt like some of the weight had been lifted off her shoulders… and put on Kelly's. That is where it should be. I was the victim. I did nothing wrong.

Kelly all of the sudden seemed to come back to reality. "Okay, I did a really, really bad thing. And you can do whatever you want to me after we get out of this thing. But right now, we are *in* this thing. We have to figure out a way to get out of here. I absolutely 100 percent know David is capable of murder. We—Kelly and Janet—represent a huge risk to him. I can't imagine any way he would let us leave this hole alive. I know I won't survive, because he had no qualms about killing Kevin, and I am just one more loose end for him. And you? You were kidnapped by me, which definitely gets me into trouble. But it also draws attention to him…. and I don't think he wants any attention pointing to him. As far as he is concerned, he got away with murder. No one would believe me if I tell them David killed Kevin. I have no proof. They have no body. They have no murder weapon. As far as the police are concerned, Kevin is in Brazil living it up with some hot Brazilian babe. You are mad. I know you are mad and you have every right to be. But you need to put that aside. We have to work together. That is the only way we are going to walk out of this alive."

Janet knew Kelly was right. If they didn't work together, David would win. Kelly, well … she was a person who had obviously been driven to this by that monster. And though she could have picked a different route, out of desperation this is the only one she could see through her rage to take. Kelly was a victim too. Just like Janet. Just like Kevin. The only really bad guy here… was David. He should be thrown into jail forever for Kevin's murder and for the repeated rapes of Kelly and for raping her. David needed to pay for his crimes. Janet and Kelly, and definitely not Kevin, could rely on the law to make sure David was punished. It was up to them.

"Okay," Janet said to Kelly. "My two sides of my brain are at odds with each other. One side wants to bring you both down. But, truthfully, I want to teach David a lesson he will never forget—that people won't put up with his shit any longer. Really, if he were a cockroach, no doubt about it I would stomp him and squish him until there was nothing left but a greasy mark on the ground. I shouldn't be insulting cockroaches; they just get into our houses to eat and poop on our food to survive. People just happen to have yummy food and cockroaches aren't potty trained. David enjoys hurting and scaring people for his own sick fun. That has got to stop."

"So, other than the one plan of tasing him down here after he sedates us, what other plan do you have?" Janet looked to Kelly for a solution. She obviously seemed to have the most scheming mind of the two of them.

"I have one other idea, but first—and this is very hard for me to ask you after knowing what David did to you—but did you confront him about it, I mean afterwards?" Kelly hated to ask Janet that question, but they both needed to share all the information they could about the whole situation, no matter how uncomfortable it might seem.

"I didn't confront him. I pretended he was right—boy, did we get drunk and the rough sex got a little out of hand. I just was afraid to go against him… I had to protect myself." Janet wondered if she had done the right thing.

"That's good. So far as David knows, you are still on his side. Right?" Kelly started to get a gleam again in her eyes.

"Right, I guess so. Except for when he saw us all snuggled together in the morning." Janet reminded Kelly that they had fallen asleep with their arms around each other.

"Well, that's not such a big deal. You can say that I wanted to hold you to make sure you didn't get up and knock me unconscious some time during the night. Okay, what if we do this… next time he comes around, you and I get into a fight? Pretend like we hate each other, that you still think I'm a psycho and that I'm still convinced you had an affair with my husband."

"Okay, what good would that do?" Janet asked Kelly. "I still don't see how that is going to get us out of this hole."

"Well, Janet… you aren't probably going to like the next part. You will have to pretend that you are hot for him, that you just can't stop thinking about the other night and how sexy it was and how crazy you both got." Kelly looked at Janet, expecting her to out-and-out reject that idea and maybe just even possibly hit her.

Janet thought for a while, and then figured out where Kelly was going with this crazy idea. "So, I say something to you like 'when I get out of here, you are dead meat' or something equally as charming?"

Kelly looked at Janet in surprise "Dead meat? Wow, you kind of scare me with how much you are getting into this. Okay. So first, we set up that we hate each other. One thought I was thinking about, was what if just before he comes to feed us again, I lay on the floor looking knocked out cold by the Taser. You could say something like, 'I grabbed her Taser and used it on her (me) while she slept.' Then you could dangle the keys in front of him. Kind of like, we are so out of here baby…. What do you think of that?"

Janet said "Ohhh… I think I'm starting to like that one. I can use all my mad acting skills and show him a little too much skin. He is so stupid… I could see him falling for it."

"See, we have options," Kelly said, smiling at Janet. "All we need to do is put our two brains together and we have more than enough brainpower to overcome anything that jackass has got in his tiny brain to pull on us. Now I am going to shut my eyes for a few minutes. If I fall asleep, wake me if anything exciting happens."

"Hah!" said Janet. "Right, gotcha." Janet didn't feel sleepy. She felt anxious. She got up and started to walk. A few hundred laps might help her burn off some of this anxiousness. Janet was, most of all, worried about her family. She thought about how they were probably worried out of their minds... wondering what had happened to her. She never went on trips by herself, really didn't even like to travel alone, so they would have known something was wrong the very first evening. I'm sure they've gone to the police. And then checked anywhere and everywhere I could have gone. Janet just hated to think about what this was probably doing to them.

Ever since her kidnapping, in the back of her mind, where she hid things from herself—feelings and emotions that she couldn't cope with without going crazy—she was more worried about her family's state of mind and fears than she was for herself. Janet had always been able to block out emotions when she really needed to, but not so with Eddie and her kids. All three of them wore their hearts on their sleeves; Janet always had to be the strong one.

She hoped that they were somehow coping, and not giving up hope, because she knew she wasn't about to give up hope. And so she took those feelings of worry and concern that she had been hiding from herself, and brought them back up to the surface, where they would do the most good. Protecting her family from hurt would force her to think faster and fight harder for her life. She couldn't let them down.

CHAPTER 16

Lunchtime came and there was another visit from their warden, David. He was all smiles. In fact, he was almost giggling, as if he was truly having the time of his life. "Hi to my favorite little pets. Pets that live in a hole in the ground. Having fun? Having a great time sharing your life stories?"

Janet shot a look at Kelly and then yelled up to David, "The only thing I want to learn about your wife's life story is about how it ends."

"Aww, bite me," Kelly blurted back at Janet. "If you don't shut your mouth, I'm going to knock your teeth into the back of your head."

"Hey, hey! Girls, girls! I thought by now bygones would be bygones, that you two would have bonded by now and become bestest friends. You looked pretty friendly this morning all cuddled together." David gave them both a big wink.

"Okay, let's get this clear. The only reason we shared space last night was because it was cold and neither of us wanted the other one to get up and kill the other one in our sleep. Your wife is a freaking psycho!" Janet stepped back a few steps from Kelly as Kelly made a couple of threatening steps toward her.

"Okay, so you need a little more time to warm up to each other. I get it. But pretty soon, you two will be cuddling like kittens. Such a sweet picture." David laughed and then walked away from the hole for a second.

"As we are very quickly running out of food, you get to share a meal today. I brought one slightly expired Lunchable thing for you two to share and one bottle of water. I think you two will need to work out how you can peacefully share. I'd hate for you to spill a drop of that precious water. See yah!" With that, David slammed the trapdoor shut and Janet and Kelly were once again alone.

"Okay, then," Kelly said with a smile. "Great acting job... you were acting ... weren't you?"

Janet punched Kelly in the arm. "Oh, I wouldn't kill you, much," and then they both broke out laughing hysterically. After a time, they both ran out of breath and the laughing stopped. But being able to share a moment and laugh in such a stressful situation seemed to refresh both of them like no night of sleeping ever could.

"Thanks. I haven't laughed like that forever," Kelly said to Janet. "Bleah, as much as I don't want to think about it, we need to get back to reality. We have a serious problem."

"We didn't before?" Janet didn't want the good mood to go away, but the look in Kelly's eyes made her realize that her cellmate was right. "Okay, you're right. The fun is over. What is our newest serious problem?"

"Well," Kelly said as she motioned for Janet to come and sit down with her on the floor. "We aren't going to be able to have much strength for much longer if we keep getting less and less food and water. We have to do something pretty quickly if we have any hope of getting out of here. And, this water bottle has been opened."

Janet grabbed the bottle from Kelly and saw that the plastic ring was separated from the lid. "Crap. So, okay... what now?"

"Well, we can assume stupid head did something with it, something either gross, revolting, evil, or all of the above. Or he could just be messing with our heads. Or he put some of the sleeping medicine in it that I conveniently left for him to use. So, we have several options. One of us could take a few sips and see if the drinker gets drugged. If nothing happens, it is probably safe to share, at least from the drugged standpoint. Not from the gross factor. Then we could follow through with the plan where one of us is drugged, which should be me because he would never trust me or let me out of this hole." Kelly stopped for a breath. The stress of the ordeal was really starting to show on her face.

"So, then I would act sexy or something and dangle the keys in his face and once he lets me out of the hole, I zap him with the Taser." Janet smiled. "Okay, I guess I could do that. The other options being?"

"Well, if he did drug the water, he would expect to show up and find us both knocked out because we had shared the same food and water. But he isn't totally stupid; he would want to see evidence that we both drank all the water and finished the food before he ventured down, which means we would have to dispose of the food and water somehow and then go without anything to eat or drink today. Which, I don't know about you, but I am so thirsty I almost... almost... could drink my own urine." Kelly gave Janet a look of sympathy, because she knew Janet had been suffering longer at her hands... a lot longer than she had. "Oh, and... he will probably have the gun with him."

"Well, our situation just seems to get more and more fun, doesn't it?" Janet felt like kicking something... or someone. "I seem to remember that I used to be a nice person, never really wanted to hurt anyone or make them mad. Well, new Janet feels like she could beat the holy living shit out of somebody."

"And if you got shot in the process? I don't want that to happen. I should never have even brought the gun. But I was so blinded by my anger that I wanted to make sure David paid. Really, I just want to hear from his mouth what he did to Kevin. And where is his body? Why did he hurt Kevin, instead of me...?" Kelly broke down sobbing.

Janet sat down beside Kelly on the floor and wrapped her arms around her. "I think I can pretty much guess to some extent how you must feel. If somebody did something to someone I love, the 'not knowing' almost would be the hardest part. I am totally with you in helping you to find out what David did to Kevin. I promise."

Kelly wiped her nose and her eyes with the back of her sleeve; toilet paper was in very short supply. "Thanks Janet, I really appreciate that. More than you will ever know. That you would even consider helping me shows me what a kind and decent person you really are. I'm so sorry I ever misjudged you."

"Well, under the circumstances... I might have done the same thing. Maybe not take as drastic steps as you did, but love makes us do crazy things. I just wish the police had paid more attention to you, taken you and Kevin's family more seriously in trying to find Kevin in the first place." Janet patted Kelly on the back. Maybe in another situation, they could have been friends, Janet thought to herself. Who knows?

"Okay." Kelly stood up with a look of determination in her face. Crying seemed to have rejuvenated her strength and her will. "I just had a crazier idea. But you aren't going to like it."

"I don't like any ideas I or anyone has had since I've been down in this pit, so.... spill." Janet looked like she was almost at the end of her rope.

"Okay," Kelly said, "maybe we've been thinking about this all wrong. There is no way he is going to be able to take one, let alone two drugged bodies up that ladder to do whatever it is he is going to do to us. So really, if he is going to rape us or beat us... or kill us, he has got to have plans on what he is going to do to us once we are drugged and he is down here. He would probably want to tie us up with the rope or something, use the handcuffs, or a combination of both. And seriously, I think he will want us to be fully cognizant of what he is doing to us when he is doing it, and making sure that the other person watches the whole thing."

"So, you aren't saying you think we should let him tie us up, are you? Because that sounds like crazy talk to me. Please don't be suggesting that." Janet felt again deflated. Maybe Kelly was crazier than she thought she was. "Okay, so then what?"

"Well, we are both going to have to pretend we are drugged, and maybe let him tie one of us up and the other one uses that time when he is distracted to make a run for the ladder. If we appear to be sleeping and we are on opposite sides of this place, he is going to want to make sure one of us is subdued before he pays attention to the other one. And he is going to want to make sure the first one he approaches (that will be me) is really out of it. So… I am guessing he might want to hit us to make sure we aren't faking."

"Oh, hell to the no!" Janet yelled. "There is no way I'm going to be able to lie there and take it while that cretin hits me—or hits you for that matter."

"See, that is the thing… we have to use that anger and whatever means necessary to save ourselves. Because if we don't use that anger, I don't think either of us is going to be able to make it out of here alive." Kelly sat down next to Janet and stared at her for a few seconds. "You do know that, don't you? If he killed one person, what is going to stop him from doing it again? We are going to be fighting for our lives. And I know you have a family who loves you and misses you and wants you back home again."

Kelly wasn't really telling Janet anything she didn't know already. Even though Janet felt she had pushed thoughts about being killed as far out of her brain as she could, she still had a hard time believing she would actually be murdered. Janet stupidly and naively had been relying on David to somehow become a human being again and let her go in the end. But really, she had to face the cold dark truth that she might die down here and her family would never know what had happened to her. And she couldn't let that happen to them. They were her world, her life… and she knew she was theirs too.

Janet looked at Kelly and nodded her head up and down. She was going to do whatever it took.

CHAPTER 17

Kelly convinced Janet to take a few sips of the water and eat half of the covered plastic meal, but only after they had examined the packaging closely and could not find any way that the seal on the food had been broken or penetrated. Kelly thought that even if the water had been messed with (which it probably had been in some way), they needed the water to keep going. If it was drugged a bit by the prescription medicine she had kept in the cabin, then the drugs might actually help, by making any pain inflicted by David more bearable and perhaps somehow making the whole nightmare of this ordeal easier to cope with.

They had a quick discussion about which was better, to get some sleep now, so they would be a little bit refreshed to deal later with whatever was to come, or to stay awake for what might come and then finally get some sleep. They both decided sleeping now—or at least resting—was a good idea, because neither of them thought sleep would come easy for them tonight.

It took Janet a while to get in a comfortable enough position on the hard concrete to relax, let alone fall asleep. She kept going over the situation in her mind, the whole thing. The chance meeting, the bank robbery, the coffee shop, the gunpoint abduction, the dark drive to nowhere, dragging David's body across the grass... and ending up in a small bomb shelter/hurricane holdout or whatever the heck this room was.

This kind of stuff just did not happen to her. Her life was ordinary. She had a normal life and kids and a husband and they were a family. Nothing dramatic ever happened to her, except maybe forgetting to put the frozen chicken out to thaw on the day that company was expected for dinner that night or she accidentally bumped into another car while trying (again futilely) to back out of a spot in a supermarket parking lot. As it was, normal life, with normal problems, was hard enough for Janet to handle. She was always told, "Oh, you need to get a thicker skin," or "Don't pay attention to that, guys always act like that." But really, when she thought about it, people were telling her to let the bad person win, why fight it? There is no point. It has always happened, it is happening, and it will always happen... no matter what anyone tried to do to stop it. No one could change what society felt was ingrained into the fabric of the way things just are.

Well, Janet thought to herself, I think I have truly had enough. Enough of putting up with people putting me down, with others taking my accomplishments and using them as their own, with people beating my self-worth down and "putting Janet in her place" only to make themselves feel better and/or advance themselves somehow.

She deserved better. She was on this Earth and just like anyone else; she had the right to claim what was rightfully hers. In this case, Janet felt what was rightfully hers (morbidly at first) was to decide how she was going to die. Death was death. No matter how much pain she endured from evil people who had never had any goodness in their hearts, in the end... would that even mean a thing? Dead is dead. Whatever comes after comes after. The pain and the hurt and the victory at the end were hers to choose. She could go down cowering in the corner... begging for her life. Or, she could confront the horror... endure whatever pain or injury or humiliation that was to happen to her... and make sure that she had respected her body and mind, her will to live, and really, at the end... make sure that she had done all she could do to protect the needs of the people who loved her. And that until the end, she had done all she could do to make it back home. After Janet felt her decisions were made, she drifted off into a blissful sleep.

When Janet woke up later, some time had passed. She was getting better at telling how much time had passed by listening to her body rather than by looking at a watch. Her body was now the only thing she had to clock the time. And now her clock was telling her that her mouth was extremely dry, she had a headache, and she had to pee. But something else had woken her up. The air seemed fresher but at the same time more fetid than it had ever been. And then she realized why.

David was down in the hole with them.

CHAPTER 18

How he had gotten in, opened the heavy trap door, slid the ladder down to the floor, climbed down it and then quietly invaded their safety? Why hadn't she heard him? Why hadn't Kelly heard him? Kelly and Janet had slept on the opposite sides of the room, as far apart as the miniscule room would let them. Not expecting David to be in the room, Janet hadn't had any forewarning... a chance to prepare herself mentally for him being there. She had opened her eyes straightway upon waking, so there was no pretending that she was still asleep.

"Well, rise and shine, Janet! You are kind of lazy taking a nap here in the middle of the afternoon, aren't you? Why don't you sit up? Please do it slowly, because I don't want to have to hurt you or anything. I mean, why ruin my fun by jumping ahead. Because I *will* hurt you... I just want to drag out the pleasure as much as I can." David's mouth was smiling, but his eyes were dark. Janet did as she was told.

When she sat up, Janet searched the room for Kelly. She wasn't in the spot where she had gone to sleep. She wasn't anywhere. He had let her out!

"Where is she...?" Janet started. David reached over and put his grimy finger to her lips.

136

"Shhhh! Oh, you're looking for Kelly, my lovely bride. Turns out, she isn't such a good friend after all. See, we kind of struck a deal, you know.... for old times' sake. For some reason, I have no idea why, she really, really, really wants to know where her white trash boyfriend is. And, as that seemed so important to her and everything, we decided on a switch. Well, actually, she suggested it—and it was such a great suggestion, which was amazing to me coming from her mouth since she has an IQ of about 42. See, she traded her boyfriend for you."

"What do you mean she traded her boyfriend for me? Is he still alive?" Janet was so bitch-slapped with all of the information that was coming out of David's mouth, she could barely think of all the things she wanted to ask—not to mention the questions that she was very afraid to learn the answers to.

"Well, I might have misled my sweet bride a little bit. I kind of let her believe he was still alive. Which would be a medical miracle if he were. Kind of hard to be alive when your body is spread out over many different parts of the beautiful states of Maryland and Delaware." David really seemed to be loving this. Never in a million years would Janet have thought that the David she had met in the Starbucks, the David she had thought she knew, wasn't even real.

"Well, I don't think Kelly would ever believe you if you said that he was still alive. They were in love. He wouldn't have just abandoned her." Janet was struggling to keep up with her thoughts and emotions that were free floating in her brain at that moment. It was as if her head were filled with millions of words, set free from their tidy brain storage compartments and now just slowly floating by her consciousness. She grasped to find any words that she could put together into a sentence.

"Well, see, Kelly so wanted her ghetto boyfriend to be alive that she was incredibly easy to dupe. The first part I told her was actually the truth. I grabbed him as he was getting out of his car near his home. I punched him in the head until he hit the ground and frankly, that guy really did not know how to take a punch. I took that opportunity to tie his hands around his back and then gagged him with a nice soft piece of burlap I had. Then, really, when he came to, with a knife pushing into his back, it was easy to get him to crawl into the trunk of his car. Just to make sure he was doubly secure on our little road trip, safety first, I tied his legs up and then created some kind of a version of a hog tie for him. I really didn't know what I was doing, should have read up on that a little beforehand... but hindsight is 20/20. Then I closed the trunk, hopped in his cheap-ass car, and drove off with him in it. Actually, I didn't think it was going to be that easy. Or take so little time. Oh well, just made my schedule a little easier."

David stopped there and looked at Janet. "You know, you are looking a little thirsty, besides being disgustingly dirty. Here, I brought you some water."

Janet took the bottle from his hand and was going to hurl it at him, but David quickly caught her hand and twisted it brutally. "I wouldn't do that, Janet. That is the last bottle, and as I was so gracious as to offer it to you.... wouldn't it be extremely rude to hit me with my own gift?" With that, David threw her arm back at her and the bottle fell out of her hand and landed on the floor.

"Here, let's try again. I am giving you water. It isn't poisoned or drugged or anything, and look... seals still on the bottle. Really, much more exciting for me to think that you will be awake for the fun we are going to have in a little bit. Well, at least *I* will."

Janet took the bottle from his hands and took a couple of big swallows. She frankly kind of hoped it was drugged. After about half a minute, with David patiently watching her, Janet could feel some of the life come back into her. Her brains started to defuzz some, and she felt like her mouth was slowly finding a way back to forming words and sentences.

"So, where does Kelly think Kevin is? I just don't buy that she would so readily believe that he had just run away." Janet felt like her head was swelling; the few sips of water really were not enough.

"Well, at the time, I told her that if she would just be quiet about you... and stuff," David smiled maliciously here, "that I would give her his address and his telephone number. I told her that I just wanted to scare him, make him rethink his whole relationship with her. I told her that I told Kevin if he didn't back off of my wife, I would kill not only her but also his sister and his parents. And then I recited their addresses to him. Actually, that was kind of brilliant of me... to make her think that I just wanted to keep Kelly and her stupid boyfriend apart to mess with their heads... and their relationship. I mean, seriously, it almost sounds like something I could have or would have done. But, I took a different route."

"So, does she or doesn't she believe that Kevin is still out there, alive somewhere?" Janet was so confused with his long-winded and convoluted stories that she was having a hard time keeping up. She kept drinking water, hoping that stalling for time would give her brain enough time to wrap around just how she was going to kill him.

"Well, sad to say.... Kelly now knows the truth. She didn't take my wallet, you know? It might have given her the balls to do what she couldn't do in the first place, seeing what I had inside. But that is Kelly for you; she always underestimates people's intelligence. Or I guess overestimates people's intelligence with regard to Kevin." David smiled, reached into his pocket, pulled out his wallet, and then pulled out a photograph.

"Here. Have a look. Kelly loved this picture of Kevin. I think she wants a poster-sized print on canvas of this beauty to put in her bedroom at night."

David leaned over and shoved the photo of Kevin into Janet's face. She did not want to look at it. She knew it would be bad... so she turned her head away and said, "No, I believe you. No thanks," which of course only made David madder still, and more insistent. He roughly grabbed her face and twisted it around so she was looking directly into his eyes.

"If I were you, sweet... sweet Janet.... I would look at this photo. Or it will only be worse for you in the end."

Janet kept her eyes closed for a few moments, hoping David would stop forcing the issue, until David shifted his hand down from her face to her neck and started to squeeze hard. Reluctantly, she opened her eyes. She couldn't believe— couldn't focus in on what she was seeing. This had to be a trick or something. The sickest, cruelest trick she had ever even imagined anyone ever doing. Because in front of her face was a picture of Kevin. A picture that was so real, she could not even wrap her mind around it by trying to pretend this was a movie or a dream and that she would wake up soon.

The picture showed a picture of a human; or rather, whatever she was seeing looked like it used to be a human at some point. It could have been Kevin, she couldn't tell. The hands and the legs of the person were tied behind his back, together barely supporting the now-diminished weight. A piece of blackened pipe held them inches above the licking flames of an open fire. Kevin was on a spit, like some dinner at a fancy exotic party where they serve a cute little used-to-be-pink whole pig, but now his skin was grotesquely cooked to a brown, crispy perfection. David hadn't even forgotten to put an apple in his mouth.

Janet immediately started throwing up. There was nothing inside of her, but that didn't matter to her stomach or to her mind. She kept heaving and spitting; her body had taken over, behaving almost with a mind of its own, maybe to protect her brain from the grisly reality of what she was seeing. After what seemed like a long time to Janet, the vomiting gradually slowed and evolved into a sort of convulsion. There was nothing more for her to push out of her body, but the sickness she felt was so intense she just couldn't stop. She didn't think she would ever stop.

"Yeah, he was a little too crispy on the outside and somewhat undone on the inside, but for a very first human roast…. I'm kind of proud. Sure you don't want to look again at the photo?" David started to move the photo again toward Janet's face and with that, Janet blanched with fear.

"What kind of animal are you? Why would you do that to another human being? It's one thing to shoot somebody or stab somebody to death.... But that? That is beyond.... Oh, I'm going to be sick again..." Janet started heaving once again, but nothing came out.

"Really? I thought it was somewhat brilliant and unique. I always like to try things a little 'outside the box,' shall we say? But then, it was like... what to do with the body? I got so excited about the pig roast that I hadn't really planned for what's next. So, I did the next obvious step: I cut him up into manageable pieces. And, because when I want to do a job, I really want to do a job well, I left him there and went out on a search for some butcher's paper. Do you have any idea how hard that is to find? I finally went to a butcher shop and told them my son-in-law had killed a deer and that the nitwit didn't have anything to wrap the deer meat in to stash it in the freezer. The butcher laughed, and then we talked about the imaginary hunting trip I had been on with my inbred non-existing son-in-law. Really a funny story, all made up of course, but I bought some butcher paper from that guy, along with four T-bone steaks. Nice guy."

David paused to take a look at Janet. "How are you doing there? You know, you can stop throwing up anytime now. It really is kind of a turnoff, if you know what I mean."

Janet shot David a glance that was apparently alarming enough for David that he backed up a step. "Okay, then. I will try to make the rest of the story as short as possible. See? I'm a nice guy. So... where was I? Oh yeah, the pig roast.

"After I got back to where I had left Kevin, a somewhat swampy area that I doubt anyone would voluntarily hang out in, I realized that I needed some more sort of a plan. I didn't want to bring Mr. Meat home to put in my freezer. So, after some more hacking with an axe and a lot of sweating on my part, I got him finally cut down into freezer sizes. And then laying each part, one at a time, onto the butcher's paper, I neatly wrapped him up and taped him closed with the masking tape… tape that the nice butcher had given me *gratis*. See, still nice people in the world."

Janet's head was pounding, she knew she shouldn't… but she took a small sip of water. She had to start thinking clearly. This depraved and sadistic nut job was beyond the scope of her imagination of what is evil. She had to find a place in her brain that was safe to hide for a few minutes. And then, to find a place in her brain that could set aside her humanity… to save herself and also… to save anyone in the future from his sick, sick, sick…. Janet just didn't know how to finish that sentence in her brain. She had run out of vocabulary.

"You better now? Can I go on?" David obviously didn't give a rat's ass about Janet's welfare, but he did want her to hear the whole story.

"Okay, so after neatly wrapping the packages, I took a little drive. I figured everyone has trash day somewhere on any given day, so… well, it took a lot of driving around through every country bumpkin neighborhood and low-rate area until I had disposed of a piece of him inside the garbage can trash bags of… I don't know… I think maybe 34 of them? Not quite sure. But he sure is spread out around the area. After that was done, I dumped his car in a swampy area that I highly doubt anyone frequents. Well, at least they haven't found it yet.

"I rinsed myself off in some quite icky swamp water, and after a few miles of walking along back roads, I sidled into Delaware City and blended in with the city folk. Really wasn't that hard. I smelled like stinky fish water, I looked like a hobo. I told someone in a local that my dinghy had split a hole in it and sunk a few hundred feet out and … again that imaginary son-in-law… always good for a back-up story (do you have any idea how many men hate their sons-in-law? There should be a support group). But anyway, I caught a ride in to the city of Wilmington with Todd… who I believe had only three teeth, maybe four. Man, he was wasted, and he really should not have been driving at all. I got dropped on a corner, jumped on a bus, and after a short walk was back in my nice clean car for the trip back home. Thank god, I had an old blanket in the trunk to sit on. I think the smell of me would have never come out of the upholstery. So, I guess that is it. The story. I don't think I'm leaving anything out."

"Where is Kelly? Did you kill her too? You might have left that little part out." Janet was furious now. If she had been alone in the world, without a family and friends who loved her and would miss her, she would have launched herself at David's neck and chewed out his trachea. But as it was, Janet didn't think her blood pressure could go much higher without bursting a vein or artery somewhere in her body.

"Oh, settle down, Mrs. *'I was abducted by a woman and imprisoned and now I actually give a shit what has happened to her.'* Geez, is there some stupid 'woman code' or something? Like 'that bitch stabbed me, but no way am I going to let that pimp of hers slit her throat.'"

Janet pulled herself together, as much as was humanly possibly she felt at this point, and said, "Just please, is she alive?"

David laughed out loud. Laughed like Janet had never heard him laugh throughout this whole ordeal or nightmare or whatever the hell it had been and had become. He laughed as if he was playing with puppies or something, which was so intensely incredibly wrong for the situation. Janet shuddered in revulsion.

"Well, last time I left Kelly, she was quite alive." David smiled and scratched the back of his head, as if he was trying to remember or something. "After luring her out of this hole—I can't believe how freaking hard that was—we walked back to her cute little shanty like the bestest of friends. Like neither of us had a care in the world. But as soon as we got inside that place and I shut the door, I slapped her so hard across her stupid face she just flew across the room. I mean literally flew. And then slumped, like she was a little dolly or something. I mean, what the hell was she thinking? That this would be a nice and sweet reunion? I would forgive her for being such a frigid bitch throughout our marriage and then ...

have the gall to fuck some idiot intern who cleans bedpans for a living?

So while she was lying there, so sweet and stupid…. I tied her up. Why, thank you, Kelly, for supplying me with this nice rope and a knife. I am much obliged since it would have been mighty hard to tie her up to that stupid water pipe in the floor without them. I mean, what the heck is that pipe there for anyway? There is no water in the building. I don't think it has ever been hooked up to anything remotely related to water. Just ended off in the middle of the room, like some rube started his job and then lost his job at the five and dime cleaning bathrooms and couldn't afford the six feet of pipe that would have at least made it outside of the building. How do people like that live so long? And why do we let them reproduce? Beyond me."

David took a few seconds, took a huge breath, and slightly closed his eyes. Like the whole of humanity was just a drain on him. Just him and no one else.

Janet felt a sense of relief that Kelly was still alive, but then immense fear for herself that she was still alive too. What horrible torture did he have in mind for her, if he was saving the best for his wife? Janet wished he had killed her the first time he had beaten her head on the floor.

CHAPTER 19

Janet was finally at the end of her rope. No, she thought, I am beyond the end of my rope and free-falling to earth … with absolutely nothing to stop my body from hurtling through space and then my life and my world stopping instantaneously as I hit the jagged rocks below. No one could save them from the monster named David. No one knew. Kelly had made sure of that. Well, Starbucks probably had a video camera somewhere in their place. But why would anyone think to look there for her? She rarely went to Starbucks … and if she did it was in the mall where she could splurge on some high-calorie, high-caffeine, fluffy girly drink to fortify herself before she continued whatever sort of shopping she had left to do.

Not that anyone would ever believe that she had driven off into the sunset. That just wasn't her style. For one thing, she would have packed the kids into the car with her. As every Mother knows, no one can raise your kids as well as Mom can. Not even Dad (sorry Eddie). And she would have at least taken some of her clothes and shoes and a few books with her. Janet again pushed her family to the back of her mind. They were the people she was staying alive for, but she couldn't spend a second feeling sorry for herself or for them. She needed, more than anything, to stay angry.

And then, Janet thought she knew just what to do: make David angry too. Angry people always did stupid things, especially if they felt like they were all of a sudden not in control of a situation. All of their plans, their time schedules, and their depraved ideas would be thrown aside as they somehow tried to retake the power that was stolen from them. And judging by David's loving attitude toward women, he would be very easy to anger. But how, exactly?

Before Janet could put any thought or logic into what or how or when she was going to do something, David finally came back to life.

"I've got another present for you, Janet. But you are going to have to guess what it is." David had a sick twisted look on his face like, *I'm a boy with a frog behind my back* mixed in with a *hey, I'm going to make you into shish-kabob* look.

Janet, pretty much knowing this would piss him off somehow said, "Um, is it bigger than a bread box?" in the most vacuous blonde-haired stereotypical voice she could come up with. Of course, she mixed it with a little bit of Valley Girl. Because, duh.

David's happy mask fell away from his face for a few seconds, but it slowly slid back on. He wanted to continue this game. Extend out his fun, as long as he could. This was his ultimate dream. Why rush it along because this stupid chick has a smart mouth? "Um, no. Mrs. Sarcastic Janet of Valley Girl Land. It is smaller than a bread box."

Janet appeared to be thinking very hard, as if now she was the dimmest female bulb on the planet. "So, it isn't a pretty airplane with pink furry seats?"

David's face and eyes kind of blanked out. It was as if the human that he was had gone away, maybe permanently. "Oh, so funny, Janet. Go ahead. Be funny. Ha, ha, ha. You are possibly the stupidest bitch on the planet if you think whatever the fuck your little plan is going to work on me." David closed his eyes for a moment and when he opened them, the blanked out look was still there, but now it was burning. Janet knew she couldn't push her luck any further.

"Okay, okay. I get it. Is it food, like some yummy Lunchable? Because, at this point, no matter how past the expiration date or how moldy it is, I would eat it in a heartbeat." Janet was pretty sure she could eat anything. Whatever. As long as it filled the giant sucking hole that was once her stomach.

"Oh, good guess Janet. Thank you for playing. But no, really sorry, it isn't food. I think I might possibly have eaten any and all of the food that my harridan fishwife had stowed in her hovel. This, I think you will like almost just as much. At least I know I will." With a giant swirl of his hands, as if he were some Vegas magician, David pulled from behind his back... a pack of baby wipes.

Normally, Janet would have been ecstatic and all over those baby wipes. Sitting down in this dank hole, either sweating or freezing, and not being able to even spare one drop of water to clean anything, she just knew she was probably covered with excrement and pee and the disgusting stench of David. But Janet knew that those wipes would come with a price.

Janet wasn't sure how to play this one. Grateful and nice, like she would usually be in a situation where someone saw that she needed or wanted something and had thoughtfully provided it for her? Or should she be snotty and reject them, scream at them and then scream at David? How could she easiest get from point A—being in this hole of death with him—to point B—being at home watching HBO encore presentations with her husband? Before she could respond, her choice was abruptly taken away from her.

"Okay, ha, ha. Janet has had her fun. David is so amused." David's face didn't even come close to portraying the descriptive words he had uttered.

"Listen, you stupid skanky bitch. You smell like you've bathed in an outhouse. Women are like "stink machines." Squatting on the ground to pee... or take a shit... doesn't matter. They always end up smelling the same. Like some whore who has had made one too many trips to the backseat of a Vega. No, not quite right. Like she has been swimming in pig shit after having too much sex in the back of a Vega."

Janet knew she reeked. At this particular moment in time, she reveled in her stink. The smell of her sweat and her body odor and even the dehydration had made her body stink rank beyond belief. Nevertheless, there really could be only one reason why David wanted her to smell less acrid: because he planned on climbing all over her with his disgusting body and his putrid breath and having David's version of "sex" with her. Janet paused for just a second. Was it worth it, to please him with this one thing?

"Listen bitch," David said, in the nicest way possible. "Here is the thing. You are going to get clean. The smart way to do it would be to nicely take the wipes like a lady, thank David profusely for his kind generosity, and then proceed to get at least one of the first layers of stink off. Or, Janet could be stupid. She could say some smartass thing to David, thereby giving David no choice but having to clean Janet himself. I don't have kids, Janet. I don't know how baby wipes are supposed to work. Do you take off only the top layer of skin? Or, if a baby is really messy, do you need to dig deeper?"

Janet leaned forward and timidly took the baby wipes out of David's extended hand. Everything in life has a fucking price, doesn't it? "Okay," she said pleasantly to David. "I seriously appreciate the opportunity to wash some of what is this hole in the ground off of me. Not like we are living in the most sanitary of situations." She glanced toward the bathroom corner and David's eyes followed suit. "Thank you. Your wife has sure left me in a pile of shit."

Janet pulled out a wipe and started to clean off her face. And for those brief few seconds, Janet closed her eyes and relished the feeling of dirt being wiped from her eyes, and mouth, and cheeks. It felt so good, but it was hard trying to pretend she was the only one in the world when a monster was standing in front of her watching her every move.

"Very good, Janet. Wouldn't want your pores to get too big; it is really not an attractive look. Make sure you clean around the front and back of your neck." Janet really didn't need him there giving her directions, but getting even a little bit cleaner, in her mind, was nirvana. After cleaning off the front and back of her neck, Janet proceeded to clean her forearms and finally her hands. She then wadded the now brown wipe in a ball and threw it toward the direction of the "bathroom."

"Thanks." She really did try to sound sincere.

"Well, Janet, you do look just a tidbit better," David nodded approvingly. "But I think you need a better washing down than that. I know how much women value their cleanliness and femininity. I think there is probably more of your body to address. Unless, that is, you want me to do it for you."

Janet closed her eyes. The first time David had touched and violated her body, she had been unconscious. This time, David seemed to want to make this some slow, sick show, to see how uncomfortable he could make her, which apparently seemed to increase his enjoyment.

"Go ahead," David encouraged. "If I were you, I'd take off my shirt first. I'm sure a fresh wipe..." he whipped a clean one out of the container... "would make you feel so much better, don't you think, Janet?"

Janet felt her skin crawl—it seemed like it would *literally* crawl—away from the sound of his voice. It just really seemed like her future was set, that there was no way in hell she was escaping this. Janet felt herself dying inside.

CHAPTER 20

A million thoughts ran in a haphazard manner through Janet's mind. How could Kelly sell her out like this? Was she stupid enough to believe that David was going to let her go after he admitted to roasting her lover and then raping (and probably killing) another woman? Janet was very reluctant to believe that even the most desperate of women would be stupid enough to believe that anything this psychopath said was even remotely true. Janet decided to play toward David's feelings of superiority. He really did think he was smart. But he's not smart, Janet thought; he's just crazy.

"So," Janet started as she kind of wiggled her body around as if she was trying to get in a better position to take her shirt off. "Left Kelly all alone up there, did you?" David looked at her from the side of his eyes. "Are you really sure she can't slip out of your 'rope' or whatever and that she isn't right now at the highway flagging down a Highway Patrol Officer?"

For a second, just a slight hesitation… Janet saw a flash of fear enter David's eyes. Bingo, Janet thought. "Because if she somehow got out… I mean… what did you tie her to? A chair? An appliance? Some pipes? Because you just never know, she could get loose in a way you hadn't even thought of.

In fact, she might just actually come over here and shut the lid down on both of us again and be done with us."

Throughout Janet's whole "what if" story, David had stood with his head turned away from her. Now David's head was again turned and he was looking straight at Janet. He had a smile on his face.

"Hmmm. That might be a little hard for her. Kelly, um, decided to put up a little fight and whoops, my knife might have accidentally gone into her side. She seemed to be losing blood pretty quickly. You know how knife wounds are— sometimes you get unlucky and accidentally hit an artery or something. So, Janet, I highly doubt that any time soon Kelly is going to be running up the road…. or dropping the door down on us. Because she did look a little 'bleedy.'"

Janet was stunned. He wouldn't do that, would he? Um, yes, a man who kills someone over an open fire probably wouldn't think twice about doing that. Nevertheless, Janet wasn't exactly sure David was telling the truth. He didn't have blood on him, as far as she could see. But, she knew now that David was capable of almost anything. She felt defeated. Why was this happening to her? She didn't deserve this. No one deserves this.

Janet decided to challenge David. "I don't believe you," she said, which turned out to be exactly the wrong thing to say.

"You don't believe me. You know what? I am getting very sick of waiting for you to take your fucking shirt off. And I am also getting very sick of listening to your fat mouth that just doesn't seem to know when to shut up. Now, quit stalling and let's get that shirt off so we can get the show on the road. You know what? Never mind. I'm getting sick of waiting." With that, David grabbed Janet roughly by her hair and slapped her face as hard as he could. "Are you going to shut up now, or do I have to slap you again?"

That violent hit to Janet's face, which left her ears ringing, brought Janet smashing down to earth to the sickening reality that there would be no way out of this. She didn't know how or what she could do to change the way things were going to happen, because they were going to happen no matter what she did. But Janet did know one thing; she knew she didn't want to die. And she really didn't want to die without her family knowing what had happened to her.

With her head still reeling from the brutal slap, Janet was in no condition to fight David off. He grabbed the bottom of her shirt and quickly ripped it up and over her head, taking a handful of hair out of her head in the process.

"Hey, nice bra! Kind of like the one my grandma would wear or something. Not really sexy, is it? Is your husband gay or something, huh, Janet? Well, then you really need what I got. I am one hundred percent man. Did my wife tell you about me? About how much of a man I really am?"

David grabbed Janet's shoulders hard and pulled her up close to his face. His breath stank of tooth rot and old cheese and something else moldy. He grabbed the back of her head and pulled his mouth up to hers to kiss, his mouth open and wet, and he rammed his tongue into her mouth, so far into her mouth that his teeth hit her teeth. It was more than Janet could take. She pushed him away from her face, trying desperately not to vomit again, which pissed off David even more. He grabbed the back of Janet's hair and pulled hard. With his other hand, he grabbed her face and squeezed her cheeks roughly with his hand.

"Don't do that again! Do you understand me, Janet? It makes me think you don't like me... and I know that isn't true. I know you are into me—you definitely were the other night. Judging by that bra, I bet you haven't had sex with anything but a vibrator in a long time. Do we understand each other Janet? Are you clear on this?"

David was squeezing Janet's cheeks together so hard, there was no way she could talk and say yes, so as much as she could, she nodded her head yes. David pulled her face toward his again, licked her check, and trailed his free hand down her face onto her throat. He then moved quickly down to her bra, shoved his hand in, and grabbed Janet's nipple, squeezing hard.

Janet tried to fight him away, but that only made him more aggressive. David looked down at her breasts with a sick, twisted look on his face. He then looked back up into Janet's face and stared directly into her eyes while he painfully ripped down the front of Janet's bra.

"Do I have your attention now, Janet?" he said. Reaching down with his hands, her grabbed both of her breasts and squeezed deliberately hard. Apparently, he was not getting the correct response from Janet, so David then moved his head down to her breasts and bit down on one of her nipples.

Janet cried out in pain. She could no longer hold back her cries, David had become so vicious and rough, and she didn't think she could survive the pain. Janet wished David would slam her head into the floor again, knock her unconscious, even if he killed her in the process. That would be a welcome relief. But David seemed to want to watch her every moment of agony; Janet didn't think there would be any relief. His hands kept moving down her naked torso, sliding down her stomach and down into the front of her jeans, and then with a final thrust he pushed until his fingers were in her panties.

Janet tried to close her mind off to the incredible pain she was experiencing, while at the same time trying to quell the quickly escalating fears of what David would do to her next. Janet increased her efforts to free herself, she scratched at David's face, trying to gouge out his eyes with her nails. When she failed at that, she hit, kicked, and bit any place she could reach to try to get him to release the grip he had on her, but he was just too strong. Janet was losing her fight when all of a sudden a deafening loud blast of noise filled the room, a sound so loud it was as if time had stopped for a few seconds. With nowhere to go in the small room, the loud sound echoed again and again off the hard surface of the walls.

Seconds or so later, Janet couldn't tell how long, she felt the weight of David's body shift suddenly. Then, abruptly, David moved away and then he was off of her. After the enormous wave of sound, the pain in Janet's body and mind was relieved some, but the new pain in her ears was soon joined by David's loud screams of pain.

Janet opened her eyes, not knowing what had just happened, or what she expected to see. As she readjusted her vision to the dim light of the room, there was a light and she saw the trapdoor was open. But the opening wasn't exactly square; a shape was blocking some of the light. Not believing what she was seeing, Janet rubbed her eyes with the back of her arm, as though when she rubbed them, the vision before her would disappear. But it didn't. It was Kelly and she was still alive!

Kelly was on the ladder, with the gun in her hand, and there was now a blank and dark stare resting in her eyes as if it had always been there. Her expression didn't change... she just stared at the floor where David lay.

Janet was the first to speak. "You shot him? Oh my fucking god, oh god, oh my god Kelly... I thought you were dead. He said he had stabbed you or I have no freaking idea what he said... I thought you were dead!" Janet was so stunned and relieved and shocked at the loud sound and the vision of Kelly on the ladder with a gun in her hand that she just sat there. Her mouth and her brain were trying to think what to say but failed miserably at the task.

"You fucking asshole," Kelly whispered quietly at David but under her breath, as if this were information that she and only she was supposed to hear. But, then Kelly said it again, this time with a furor in her voice that was unmistakable. "You fucking asshole!" Janet was stunned. Kelly had transformed from a dead-eyed deer in the headlight look into a look that Janet almost wanted to call... hungry?

Kelly swiftly shifted her eyes to Janet and screamed, "Hurry up Janet. Get to the damn ladder and move. Now!"

Janet did not have to be told twice; she wanted out of this place more than anything else she had ever wanted in her life. She grabbed her shirt up off of the floor and tried to stand up, wobbly at first but then with more determination. Janet felt like she couldn't get to those wooden rungs fast enough. Before she even registered taking a step, Janet was on the rung below Kelly, wishing she could crawl over the top of her and escape out of this fucking hole that had buried her alive for who knew how long.

Kelly could feel Janet's urgency. With one eye on David, who was still screaming and clutching his leg, Kelly climbed up the ladder and stepped off and out onto the ground above. Almost stepping on her to get over the top of her, Janet reached the top of the ladder and the ground and the dirt and the blinding sunlight and wanted to keep moving, keep running until every thought, feeling, and abuse she had endured these last couple days were cleared from her mind. She was free!

CHAPTER 21

Never had the air smelled so sweet and fresh. The fresh smell of the pines, the more subtle smell of the grass, warmed in the late afternoon sun, rose up to greet Janet's nose, and as she inhaled, her body was filled with its clean and somehow peaceful scent. Janet thought she had never smelled anything as sweet as this. And the sun, the beautiful, blinding sun... so bright she couldn't fully open her eyes, seemed to caress her skin and her hair with warmth. Could the sun be the very essence of love? At this moment in time, Janet felt it was. The blue sky... and the birds. Janet couldn't believe in such a short time that these wonderful things, these beautiful things she took for granted every day, should at this moment make her feel more beautiful and loved than she had ever felt and happy, extremely happy that she was alive to experience it.

It seemed to Janet that things around her were going in slow motion and that she was experiencing every sensation together at once. Nature itself had made Janet's senses so in tune with it that she didn't hear Kelly yelling. Didn't hear Kelly slowly saying her name louder and louder, finally escalating into a scream.

"Janet. Janet! Janet... get your ass over here and help me with this." Janet slowly swiveled her head to look at Kelly and took in the totality of their situation in one glance. Everything registered. Kelly struggling first to close the lid... and then struggling to keep it closed as a force from below was pushing up, trying to escape. She could see the sweat running down Kelly's face, the grimacing pain evidenced in the set of her jaw, and further down her body... a blossoming of red grew larger by steps on the shirt she was wearing. He had stabbed her.

Seeing the blood brought Janet more swiftly back to earth than any sound or sight could. She rushed over to Kelly's side and put the full weight of her body on top of the door to the dungeon below. The door was bucking up and down, lifting up the weight of both Kelly and Janet, while David screamed in a rage down below. David must have been functioning on full adrenaline at that point. Janet didn't see how a man who had been shot in the leg, who was standing on the rung of a ladder could push so hard against gravity and the strength and the weight of the two women combined.

Kelly reached her hand up to her forehead and tried to wipe some of the sweat off it, sweat that looked to be getting into her eyes, but her effort only managed to mix dirt in with the sweat, which gave her a look like she was some sort of feral version of herself or something.

Kelly once again barked orders into Janet's ears. "Get the wheelbarrow. Janet, go over, get the stupid wheelbarrow, and roll it over here on top of the door. Hurry, I can't hold him by myself much longer."

Janet looked around, searching the area, and finally noticed that a rusty wheelbarrow, filled almost to overflowing with wood, was sitting about three feet from where they were. So this was how the door was reinforced. Janet knew that if they had eventually even reached the door above their underground room, it would have been nearly impossible to force the door open. The door had been weighted down. They wouldn't have escaped.

Janet quickly headed over to the wheelbarrow and grabbed the handles. The wheelbarrow was so heavy, the handles so splintered, the metal so rusty, Janet didn't understand how it could stay in one piece. But with a will born of anger and frustration, Janet somehow managed to push the rickety wood-filled wheelbarrow over and onto the top of the door. As the door finally eased down and stayed closed, Kelly grabbed a hasp attached to the door and jammed it onto the metal circle on the frame. A thick stick was nearby, and she finished the job of securing the door by pushing the stick into the metal circle of the closure, effectively trapping David inside.

Janet slumped down in a heap beside Kelly. After the initial joy of having finally crawled out of that hole and then the physical exertion of pushing the wheelbarrow even a few feet so they could get the door closed and regain their safety, Janet was now exhausted beyond words. Well almost.

"I have never, well almost never, felt so happy, tired, dirty, smelly, angry…. and then back again to happy before in my life ever." Janet smiled in relief and in joy. She was so wrapped up in the last few minutes of finally being outside, she hadn't but for a brief moment looked at Kelly. Now, Janet searched out her eyes, wanting to connect with her and somehow share in the joy she was feeling at the moment. But Kelly's eyes were squeezed shut in pain.

"I'm sorry, Janet. I am so truly deeply sorry for what I've done to you… what I have put you through. You could have kicked my ass back down into that hole with my evil monster of a husband. But you didn't." Kelly opened her eye, took a deep breath, and turned to look straight into Janet's eyes. "A lot of people would have in your situation. After what I had done to you first and then allowed to happen to you, I would probably have been one of those people who would have kicked me into the hole, locked the bolt, and walked away forever. But you didn't. Thank you, Janet. Thank you, I don't deserve it… but thank you."

Janet didn't know what to say. So, she did the only thing she could think to do. She reached over, put her arms around Kelly, and with that hug, Janet started to cry. She felt like she would never stop crying again, the pain and the fear of the last few days were finally being released from her body. Janet was so happy just to be alive, that the details of all the horrible things that had happened to her had been driven to the furthest back of her mind. Kelly had started to cry too, first just a few sniffles and then she became a blubbering mess like Janet. They sat like that, their arms around each other and crying together. They both felt like they had lost so much and because of that, their shared relief turned into an immutable kind of bond. The finger pointing would come later... or not. Human compassion was now all that mattered to either of them. That was all they needed.

CHAPTER 22

"Man, I could use some tissues, how about you?" Kelly pulled away from Janet and having no other choice, wiped her eyes and her nose on her sleeve. "Oh, and a bath."

Janet laughed a little and did her best to clean off some of the mess the crying probably had done. Or, maybe it had made her face look better, she didn't know. Janet was scared to look in a mirror. She probably didn't look human at this point.

"I can't wait for a bath. And then a shower. And then another bath. And then a 24-hour nap snuggled under clean sheets with my pillow under my head in my nice warm bed." Janet slowly made it to her feet and brushed some of the dirt off of her pants with her hands... or wiped some of the dirt off of her hands onto her pants. They were equally dirty. Then looking to Kelly she said, "You're bleeding."

"Yes, courtesy of my husband." Kelly looked down at the front of her shirt and for the first time since the rescue attempt, saw all the fresh blood. "I wrapped it up the best I could, guess it wasn't enough? After the bastard sliced me with the knife, the sight of the blood and everything, I must have passed out. When I came to, David wasn't there anymore. He probably thought, no, probably *hoped* I was dead or soon would be. Somehow I got over to my bag and pulled out of it the only two somewhat clean things I had left, a pair of underwear and some knee socks. I did my best to bandage the stab wounds, but not very well I guess. I think my makeshift bandages slowed down the bleeding some at first, but now it looks like in the interim I've managed to make it start bleeding again."

"We need to get you to a doctor." Janet was starting to be very concerned about Kelly. Her face was pale and was getting paler by the minute. Janet thought Kelly was going into shock. "Is there a phone or anything?"

"Phones are long dead." Kelly said through the pain, pain that had reignited as she shifted positions to try to get more comfortable. "In the house, I have a bag. Could you get it for me? I have—at least I hope I still have—some acetaminophen in it that might help the pain some."

"Absolutely," Janet said to Kelly. Just the thought that she could now do something to help Kelly made Janet's brain travel back to the present, back to the right here and now. Swiveling her head around, Janet saw a small rickety cabin about 75 yards away. "I'll be right back," she said toward Kelly, then made her way through the uneven field and over to the door of the cabin as fast as she could manage.

Janet felt like her body had aged 20 years in a few days. Every little muscle and bone ached and she felt so weak that a couple of times during the short walk she got woozy and thought she might pass out. But she made it to the door and slowly opened it.

The cabin, or shack really, was basically just one room. Inside there was very little, as there was only room for very little: a cigarette-burned table, one chair, one cabinet, and a sink, which served as the kitchen. Across the very small room, there was an old woodstove and on the floor next to it, a sleeping bag and a pillow. This place was really not that much better (or bigger) than the one she had just escaped from, but in Janet's eyes she felt like she had finally taken a tiny step back into the human race.

Next to the foot of the sleeping bag was what must be Kelly's purple bag. Janet grabbed the bag. It felt light; there really wasn't that much in it. She zipped it shut anyway and looked around the room. The cabin was extremely bare of any objects, except for the cabinet and sink and a bag of what must be garbage in the corner. After picking up the bag, she crossed over to the sink and tried the tap. Of course, no water. She opened the cabinet and it was empty, except for some cobwebs and some old yellow checked peeling contact paper. There really was nothing here. As she headed toward the door, Janet turned back around and crossed back to the sleeping bag and pillow. She would need these; she had to get Kelly warm.

The trip back to where Kelly was sort of semi-reclined on the ground was easier going this time. Janet's muscles seemed to stretch a bit, and the fresh air was starting to make her head feel a little clearer. But she was still desperately thirsty and hungry. She knew she needed something to drink quickly or things would go from crazy bad to extremely crazy bad in a hurry. Reaching the spot where Kelly was trying to rest, Janet dropped the bag on the ground next to her, close to her where she could reach it, and started to unzip the sleeping bag. When it was fully opened, Janet draped it over Kelly's shoulders as best as she could.

Kelly found a bottle of acetaminophen in her bag and shook it. A brief rattling noise told her that David hadn't taken all of it yet. She opened the lid... two left... and she held the bottle directly up to her mouth, shook both of the pills in, and started chewing. Even though she had pre-chewed the pills, Kelly still appeared to have a hard time swallowing them, but eventually she got them down.

"Thanks," Kelly said to Janet. "Okay, just give me a few minutes and we can go over a few things... and I will answer a few questions for you. But first, I need you to go retrieve the car keys from where I hid them. Can you do that?"

The car keys. The car. Her car. They had transportation. They could just hop into the car and get far away from here. Thank God.

"You hid the keys? When?" Janet asked inquisitively. Kelly shook her head in the affirmative.

"I didn't know how things would turn out. I knew that if David somehow overpowered me, he would kill us both and then take your car back to his old life and forget we had ever existed. So I hid them, almost the first day we got here. The only keys that I ever brought down into the hole with me are, I guess, your house keys?"

"Well, thank God you hid the car keys when you did, or David would be long gone by now. He must not have found them. Where are they? " Janet was up and ready to fetch. She couldn't wait to get back into her car, start it up, and leave this place far behind.

"Across that field, through the tall grass, there are a couple of wild rosebushes. They aren't too far away, kind of in that direction," Kelly pointed over to the left. "You can't see the bushes from here; they are down in a sort of a little washout or something. Actually, the rosebushes will probably find you first. Lots of stickers, that's how I found them. Next to the bushes, there is a small darker round gray rock. The keys are buried a little ways under the rock in the dirt."

"Um, okay. I'm going to go look. So, this way?" She indicated the direction Kelly had pointed toward. "Okay, I will try to find them and get back here as quick as I can."

Janet started off and was just a few feet away when she was walking through almost knee-high grass that filled the field around them. A couple of times Janet tripped in her haste, failing to see rocks and holes that the tall grass obscured from her view; she could barely see her feet. After the third time of nearly falling face first, Janet slowed down and proceeded with more caution, splitting time between staring at her feet and scanning around her to see if she could see the rose bushes. Janet was really starting to feel like she had maybe somehow steered herself off course of the straight line she was trying to follow.

She turned around to look toward where Kelly was and then guesstimated that she was still almost heading in the right direction. All of a sudden, the field started going down in a barely noticeable slow descent. Janet looked ahead; about 10 feet away, a couple of scraggly rose bushes stood, still with a couple of yellow flowers on them. The flowers made Janet smile. She had found the rose bushes. Now, the rock. After going around the bushes several times, looking underneath the branches as best she could, she finally spotted a dark rock about 12 inches into the thorny mess.

Ignoring the thorns that were scratching her hand and arm, she slid the rock to the side and with the tips of her fingers started to dig a little hole. The keys weren't buried that deep, they had just enough dirt to cover them. Janet laughed, and then said a quiet but jubilant "yes." Okay, keys found. After slowly backing her way out of the rose bushes, trying hard not to get even more scratched, Janet slowly stood up and then made her way back to where Kelly was.

Kelly had wrapped the sleeping bag totally around her body and was lying on her side, head on the pillow. Uneasily, Janet noticed Kelly seemed very still. Oh Jesus, Janet thought. Please don't let her be dead.

"No, I'm not dead yet…. just resting and trying to get warm. Please tell me you found the keys." Kelly opened her eyes and turned to meet Janet's.

"Yep, found them right away. Just where you said they would be. And the stupid bushes only scratched me about a dozen times. So, the car? I'm guessing the best idea would be for me to drive it over here and put you into it. You look in no shape to walk."

"Okay, thanks," Kelly said weakly. "I won't move a muscle."

Janet smiled and quickly turned and headed back to the cabin. Since Kelly hadn't said where the car was, and there obviously were very few places to hide it, Janet wasn't surprised to walk around to the other side of the cabin and find her car hiding there.

"I love you Mr. Car," Janet said with a big smile on her face. She unlocked the doors, climbed in, and took a deep breath. "Please, God, please... please... please let Mr. Car work." Janet put the key in the ignition, closed her eyes, and turned the key slowly. To her relief, the car started right away. Janet looked up and said a little "thank you" to God and then put the car in gear, backed up, and started the drive over the grassy terrain to where Kelly was waiting. As soon as she pulled up, she put the car in park, but left the engine running as she jumped out and went to a side door closest to Kelly and opened it up.

"Okay, now we have to somehow get you in without hurting you anymore. Think you can stand?" Janet looked at Kelly, hoping Kelly had just a little bit of strength left in her so she wouldn't have to drag Kelly into the car unaided. Janet didn't think she was strong enough at this point to get Kelly up and into the car on the back seat on her own.

Kelly gave Janet a look. A very strange look, one that Janet didn't recognize. Then to Janet's surprise, Kelly said, "Just shut the car off for a few moments. I want to talk to you about a couple of things first."

Janet gave Kelly a look as if she really believed she had finally gone crazy. "Are you kidding me? You need to get to a doctor. I want to get back to my family who are probably worried sick.... And you want to stop and have a little talk?"

"Please?" The look in Kelly's eyes told Janet that this was very important to her. Janet reluctantly went back over to the driver's side, shut off the car, and then closed the door. With that done, Janet walked over and sat on the hard ground right next to Kelly.

"Okay.... what?" Janet couldn't believe that Kelly thought now was the time for chitchat. But if Kelly really wanted to talk to her for a few minutes, would that really be such a big deal?

Janet guessed they could afford a short rest to talk; she could use a few minutes to catch her breath.

Kelly coughed a few times and gingerly pulled herself up more into a sitting position, first trying by herself and then with help from Janet. "Okay, first.... I know there aren't enough sorries in the world that could come out of my mouth to make up for the shit I've put you through. But seriously, I never thought everything through clearly enough; I was so determined to find out what had happened to Kevin. I never thought it would go this way. That David would go so far, that things could go so horribly wrong. I just wanted to scare David into telling me where Kevin was. That was all I wanted." Kelly looked at Janet, pain crossing her eyes and her face.

"I know now that Kevin is dead. That David killed him and he is never coming back. What David did to him, what he did to Kevin, was barbaric, so beyond anything I ever thought he would do. I knew David was evil, but if I had known how really evil to the core he truly is, I never would have stuck you into that hole with him. I hope you know that. I'm not that kind of person. And that picture...."

Janet stopped Kelly there. "You don't have to talk about the picture. I saw it. David forced me to look at it and then he bragged about what he had done. There has to be a special place in hell reserved just for him. I am sure of that."

"Yeah." Kelly rubbed a couple of tears from her eyes. "It's all my fault. I should have reported David to the police when he first beat me. I should have left him. I should never have brought Kevin into my life... and then fallen in love with him. If it hadn't been for me, Kevin would still be alive and you would be at home with your family. And the things David did to you... this whole damn thing is my fault." Kelly had a look on her face like someone who had just realized they had been defeated and just like that had had an important part inside of them die.

"It isn't your fault, Kelly. I mean, you could have made different decisions, taken different paths. But you weren't thinking clearly at all. David mentally abused you, he beat you, and he raped you, for years. That is what he did to you. That is definitely not your fault. And what David did to Kevin... I'm sure in your worst nightmares you couldn't have thought that David was capable of something like that." Janet reached out, grabbed Kelly's hands, and held them warmly in hers.

"You were just as much of a victim as Kevin was, and as I was. And really it isn't your entire fault. You didn't make David an animal. David made himself one. Or has always been one. Who knows?"

"I know. Part of me inside knows. But the guilt is just eating me up inside. I feel like I have nothing left inside of me that feels normal anymore. It's as if I'm just a shell of the person that I used to be, way before David came into my life. I used to be a really happy person... I used to have lots of friends. Did you know I was even homecoming queen at my high school?"

Janet smiled at that. "Well, I would have hated you from the start if I had known that." Kelly smiled at Janet's joke, a smile that quickly vanished, and her face returned to a look that was sad and then finally to inconsolable.

"We could have been bestest frenemies." Kelly tried to keep up the lightness of the conversation. But she neither had the strength or the heart left in her to keep it up. Then a wall went up, and the Kelly who was just sitting there—the Kelly who had been talking with Janet about the past few days, even doing a tiny bit of joking—quickly morphed and became deadly serious. "I'm not getting in that car with you."

"What?" Janet couldn't believe what she has hearing. "Why the hell not? You need to get to a hospital. You need to get well. You need to tell Kevin's family and the police what happened to him."

Janet stopped, finally realizing what the implications of Kelly's going to the police would be. They would eventually get the whole story, how Kelly had kidnapped her and David, how Kelly had hit her and abused her and kept her captive. They would hear about how Kelly "allowed" her crazy husband to rape Janet.

As a mountain of thoughts rushed through Janet's mind, Kelly once again grabbed Janet's hands and looked straight into her eyes. And Janet knew: Kelly wasn't going to be going back. She had nothing to go back for.

"I'm staying here. I am going to guard the entrance to this hole, to make sure that monster never gets out. Beyond that, you need to do what you need to do. You have to report this all to the police, every last bit. I don't deserve any special treatment. What I did was beyond bad. And David—he deserves to be locked away in jail, preferably one with people who are as depraved as he is, where he will hopefully suffer at the hands of his fellow inmates every day for the rest of his life."

Kelly stopped and closed her eyes for a few moments. All this talking was taking a lot out of her. Her face was ashen and it looked as if just sitting up was starting to be a problem for her. After about half a minute, she continued.

"I know I have no right to ask anything of you. But I need to make sure that Kevin's family knows what happened to him. As horrific as it is, they need to know. I'm sure the police will tell them eventually, but maybe only part or maybe all of what David did to Kevin. And I want you to tell Kevin's parents and sister about Kevin and me. How we loved each other. How he saved my life. Try to make them understand, if you ever can, why I did the things I did. Anything they want to know. However hard it may be for them to hear, I want them to hear the details of the story from you. Not some police officer or District Attorney, or whoever tells these sorts of gruesome things to family members. You know. I think above all people, you know better than anyone. You know what was going through my mind for months after Kevin disappeared. And you definitely know what sort of sadistic creature David really is.

"Kevin's parents and his sister and I have become very close since Kevin's disappearance. I don't want them to think that I was crazy or that I didn't know what I was doing. I want them to know I was just trying to somehow create a shitty closure for myself, for everything that happened to me and to Kevin.

"In my bag, in the zippered part on the side... you will find Kevin's parents and sister's names and their addresses and phone numbers. Please take it. Do what you can to help them understand, what you feel comfortable telling them, what you feel comfortable sharing with them. If not right away, maybe later when you have had the time and the distance to talk. And if you can't or never want to talk to them, I understand. Horrific things have happened. For your own sanity, you just might need to lock them up in your brain and never let them out again. I know all about that. I've been doing it to some extent for years."

Janet just sat quietly for a few minutes and tried to take in all Kelly had said to her and what she had asked her to do. The only thing Janet knew she was sure of was that she wasn't sure what she would do. First and foremost, in her mind, what she wanted most to do was to see her family again. Beyond that.... she had no idea what she should do. Her mind was blank about that part. Maybe once she was back again with the people she loved, she could reach out to Kevin's family and help them with their grief. Janet looked at Kelly, and then impulsively stroked her hair for a while and then touched the side of her cheek.

"I will Kelly. I don't know what or how or when... but they will hear from me. What happened to their son and brother and your friend and lover should never have happened. I want to tell them anything or everything. Not just for you, but partially for me too."

Kelly smiled. "That's good. I want you to heal first. And, whatever you can do, thanks. You have no idea how much that means to me." Kelly gave Janet's hand a final squeeze and then all of a sudden Kelly seemed to switch gears in her brain.

"One last thing...."

"Oh no, let me guess.... you want me to make sure Julia Roberts plays you in the movie version."

With that, Kelly started laughing again. They both were laughing. What a freaking ridiculous world they lived in. Like any of that shit mattered, the extraneous things that at one time seemed so damned important. Life mattered, here and now mattered. Happiness and family mattered.

"Okay, no... I think Julia Roberts is a little too much. Just pick some ordinary person, just like me, who can honestly portray me and how I feel right at this moment. Like my whole world has been ripped away from me, taken away by a man who I married and who I thought at one time loved me."

Janet smiled again. "Okay, what is my last thing?"

Kelly pointed to the wheelbarrow that was sitting a few feet in front of her. Could you bring some of that wood over closer to me and build me a fire... to keep me warm? I'm awfully cold."

Janet looked toward the wheelbarrow and then at Kelly. Brief thoughts passed through Janet's mind, but she quickly shoved them aside. Kelly wanted a fire to warm her. She would build Kelly a fire.

"Okay, as long as I don't have to rub sticks together. Do you have matches, lighter, paper? I'm not that much of an outdoorsy 'know how to make a fire' kind of girl. I just turn up the thermostat."

Kelly reached into her bag. "I have still, thankfully, just the thing." She pulled a plastic lighter out of her bag. "There is a notebook full of paper. And don't worry, I will coach you through how to make a camp fire."

Kelly reached inside the bag, pulled out Kevin's parents and sister's information, and gave it to Janet. "Please keep this safe. And only do what feels right for you. Whenever. You owe me nothing."

Janet took the paper and slipped it into her pocket. "Okay, I guess we're going to need some wood. I'd better fetch some."

Most of the wood was neatly chopped into fireplace-sized wedges. Janet figured Kelly had picked up the wood locally, from someone who had a hand-painted sign that read "Wood For Sale" in their yard. Janet couldn't imagine Kelly cutting all this wood up by herself. Janet grabbed a few pieces from the wheelbarrow and brought them over to a spot about three feet away from where Kelly was in her sleeping bag. After a few trips back and forth, Janet looked to Kelly.

"So, just tell me when you think there is enough."

Kelly looked at the wheelbarrow and then at Janet. Janet looked and thought to herself, what the hell. I could just wheel the whole damn thing over. Looks like it is going to get cold out here pretty fast.

Janet looked back at Kelly. "I'm just going to bring all the wood over. You never know how much you will need." Janet walked again over to the wheelbarrow, which now seemed as light as a feather compared to what it had been when she first pushed it. Janet slowly pushed it over close to Kelly and then stopped. "Can you reach the wood?"

Kelly thought for a second. "Maybe you could just dump it where I can reach it more easily? Every time I move, I feel like I am being stabbed again and again."

Janet, who was really trying hard to continue to be the nice person she was, politely did what Kelly asked. She backed up the wheelbarrow and then moved it closer to Kelly, but not so close that the wood would fly up and hit Kelly when she dumped it. When she tipped it, the wood fell to the ground with a giant crash. Really, it should definitely be enough wood to last her throughout the night…. At least in Janet's "un-camping girl" mind.

"Okay, what next?"

"Okay, rip the pages out of the notebook and you and I are going to scrunch them up in balls, so they burn slowly and hot enough for them to make the wood catch fire."

Janet, with some difficulty at first, ripped all the pages out of the notebook and passed the paper to Kelly. "While we start our paper-scrunching craft project, you can tell me all about how to put together a fire."

Kelly grabbed a sheet of paper and started scrunching. "Okay, take some of the smaller pieces of twigs and grass and stuff from the pile and set that aside. Then I need you to make kind of a teepee out of the wood. Once that's done, stuff the kindling underneath to protect it from the wind so that when it catches fire, it will be able to start the bigger pieces of wood on fire."

Janet thought back to the old westerns she had seen as a kid. With that picture in her head, she took about 12 pieces of wood and tried to make a standing teepee out of them. What she ended up making was a haphazard mess. "I think I suck at teepee making," Janet remarked. She shoved the extra wood closer, within reaching distance for Kelly, so she would be able to stick more wood on the fire when it started getting low. Then, as Kelly instructed, Janet tucked the smaller branches and twigs and some grass in a sort of bird nest fashion underneath the wood in several places.

"How is that?" Janet looked to Kelly, hoping Kelly would think it was the best campfire assembly she had ever seen and she wouldn't have to redo it.

"Perfect," Kelly said, and showed Janet all the paper that she had already scrunched into balls. "Now, I need you to put a couple of balls of paper in and under the wood pile, next to the little twigs and stuff. Then all you need to do is set the paper on fire, and nature should do the rest."

Janet took the paper balls from Kelly and jammed them in under the wood. Kelly handed the lighter to Janet and said, "All right, let's hope this works."

Janet took the lighter and after a few flicks, it lit up. Leaning into the pile of wood she had just built, Janet held the flame up to a piece of paper. It caught fire immediately. Just as Kelly said, within minutes, the sticks and kindling had caught on fire and now the larger wood was catching fire.

"Congratulations on your first campfire. You must have a gift." Kelly smiled at Janet, already luxuriating in the heat given off by the growing fire.

"Okay, anything else I need to get you before I go? Some ice cream, a container of chocolate frosting, a spoon?" Janet was teasing, but she really wished there was something else she could do for Kelly before she left.

"Um, there is one more thing. I want you to open the hatch. David and I are due for a little talk."

"What? Are you kidding me? You actually want to talk to him? Why? Just great. Oh, and of course, when I open that door, David will be right there at the top of the ladder just waiting and he will grab me. Please don't ask me to do this!"

Kelly reached into her bag and just said, "Here, take this," as she handed the gun to Janet. "Ever used one before?"

Janet looked at the gun and then she looked at Kelly. Although she had no freaking idea why, she decided to do this for Kelly, open the damn hatch, what the hell. And strangely enough, just last year on a whim she and Eddie had gone to one of those indoor shooting ranges and "killed" some paper bulls-eyes. "Yeah, I've shot a gun a couple of times. Anything special I should know about this one?"

Kelly put her hand on the gun and flicked a switch. "Not really. I've just taken the safety off. Just point and shoot. But please don't accidentally shoot your own foot."

Janet took the gun from Kelly. It felt cold and a lot lighter than the gun she had used at the shooting range. It almost felt like a toy gun. "Okay, stupid as this is, I'm going to open the door."

All of a sudden, Kelly stopped her. "Just wait a second. I want to make sure I'm armed... just in case." Kelly reached for one of the pieces of wood that was in the fire and carefully pulled it out. With the piece of still flaming wood in her hands, Kelly said, "Okay, I'm ready."

Janet took a deep breath and pulled the stick out of the hasp of the latch and then slowly pulled it back, fully expecting the door to fly up at any second. But it didn't. Janet reached over; with the gun pointed in the general direction of where she thought David would be standing, she started to open the hatch.

Just as Janet had predicted, David had been waiting for this moment. The lid quickly flew open, and as it did, the door hit Janet's hand as she held the gun. A shot went off, the bullet flying wildly somewhere out toward the cabin.

Kelly took the piece of wood she had been holding, leaned forward, and poked it into David's neck. The fire started David's shirt on fire, the flames lapping up into David's face.

David screamed in pain. He was on fire and began crazily slapping at his shirt trying to put the fire out. As David flailed about, he lost his footing on the ladder, slipped down, and hit the floor hard. Janet took this second to retrain her gun on David. She wouldn't miss him this time.

"You stupid crazy bitches. You burnt me. You fucking burnt me." David was back on the floor, livid and obviously in a lot of pain. He didn't know whether to pay more attention to his leg, which was still bleeding from where Kelly had shot him earlier, or to the new pain of freshly burnt skin around his neck and face.

Janet aimed the gun, and finding within herself a part of her that she didn't know existed, started shooting down into the hole. Not at David, but at the ladder… shooting it again and again until she ran out of bullets. The bullets had amazingly mostly hit their mark. The ladder kind of slithered down a little bit and then went crashing to the floor, falling into pieces as it landed. Janet was shaking like a leaf.

Kelly slowly reached over, took the gun from Janet, and then took a few moments to look down into the hole to see what her shooting had done. "Good job, Janet; you've killed your first ladder."

Janet looked at Kelly, her mouth opening and closing as if she couldn't remember how to form words. "I just killed a ladder." And then she laughed. There was no way David was ever going to be able to put that ladder together again. He was now definitely and completely trapped.

Janet looked at Kelly and they both smiled, sharing a moment of triumph and happiness. But then Kelly got very serious. "Okay, Janet. I've got it from here. You can go now."

Janet pulled herself out of the trance she had been in. She could go home. Janet immediately thought about her family, about how good it was going to be to see them again, to hug them and never let them go. But first, before her homecoming, she needed to go to the police.

Janet smiled wildly and said to Kelly, "Thelma and Louise." Kelly smiled back and then they shared a quick hug.

"Take care of yourself," Kelly said to Janet.

"I will. I will get help back to you as soon as I can. Main road, should I turn right or left?"

Right," said Kelly, and then quietly added, "Thank you for helping me to finally find out what happened to Kevin. And, try not to hate me for the rest of your life. You deserve to be happy."

Janet smiled. "Thanks," she said, and gave a little wave before she turned around and walked back to the car. After starting the car, she rolled down the window and said, "I will send someone as quickly as I can."

Kelly just smiled and then turned away, putting her hands up to warm them by the fire. Janet, after fumbling for a few seconds, as if she had somehow forgotten how to drive, finally got the car in gear and started driving away. Toward freedom.

As she drove, Janet reached up and adjusted the rear view mirror so she could look back. In the mirror, she saw Kelly reach into the fire, take a piece of flaming wood, and turn and drop it into the hole. Janet thought she heard something that sounded like a muffled scream.

"Just the wind," Janet said, and after looking into the rear view mirror one more time, she pushed it up toward the ceiling. She wasn't looking back. She was going home.

ABOUT THE AUTHOR

Born and raised in Plentywood, Montana, which is located in a cold and secluded part of the upper northeastern corner of the state, Trina Ator Ernst read books during the long winters... lots of them.